THREADS OF WORDS: A COLLECTION OF SHORT STORIES

ARSHIYA MITTAL

Made with ♥ on the Notion Press Platform
www.notionpress.com

To all who find refuge in the art of storytelling,

This collection is for you.

In a world often drowned in noise,

You seek solace in the quiet power of words.

May these tales offer you a moment of peace,

And rekindle the belief in the transformative magic of stories.

With heartfelt appreciation,

Arshiya Mittal

Contents

Acknowledgements

All the writings are unique and authentic and not copied from any other sources. I tried my best to make this book filled with wonderful writings which are original and covering almost all the thoughts.

Preface

I am a writer overflowing with a multitude of words. Since the tender age of 14, I embarked on a remarkable journey of penning down my thoughts. Writing has become an intrinsic part of my being, fueling my passion and guiding my creative endeavors.

With an expansive repertoire, I have ventured into various themes, fearlessly exploring the realms of politics, love, heartbreak, and beyond. My poetries encapsulate the essence of these diverse subjects, providing readers with a kaleidoscope of emotions and perspectives.

Throughout my writing career, I have been blessed with numerous achievements. From academic triumphs to securing top positions in national poetry competitions, my dedication and commitment have been recognized and celebrated. These accomplishments have propelled me forward, inspiring me to reach even greater heights.

As an accomplished author, my published works include "The Passages of Life," "Express Your Thoughts," "DNA of Innovation," "Wings," and "Whispering Poetries". Each book is a tapestry of inspiring and unique poetries, crafted with the intention of igniting a spark within the reader's soul.

My dedication and talent have garnered prestigious accolades, such as being a National and World record holder, Forever star India "Real super women" award , a recipient of the Karamveer Chakra White medal, and an honorable awardee under the esteemed A.P.J Abdul Kalam Sir International Golden Awards, where I was recognized as the "Best Writer of the Year 2021."

With unyielding determination, I strive to touch hearts, provoke thoughts, and inspire positive change through the power of words. It is my sincerest hope that my writings continue to resonate with readers, leaving an indelible mark on their lives.

Within the pages of "Threads of Words," readers will embark on a transformative journey through a tapestry of captivating tales.

This collection celebrates the profound impact of storytelling, showcasing how narratives can transcend the ordinary and touch the depths of our souls. Each story invites readers to explore diverse worlds, encounter unforgettable characters, and experience the magic that words can weave. Dive into these compelling narratives and rediscover the timeless power of storytelling.

Prologue

In these pages, you'll encounter tales that stir the heart and spark the imagination. Each story unfolds a new world, full of surprises and profound moments. Let these words take you on a journey through unexpected adventures and unforgettable characters.

1

Threads of Friendship

The storm had come out of nowhere. It wasn't supposed to rain that day in Greenwood. The sky had been clear when *Aditi* and her childhood friends *Arjun, Vikram, and Rohit* decided to reconnect.

It had been years since they last met, and their lives had drifted in so many directions. Aditi had watched them all grow into different people some better, some colder, some harder. But still, despite everything, she had clung to the hope that the bond they shared would remain untouched by time.

They had spent their childhood running wild in the woods behind their school, telling each other everything, laughing together until their sides ached, and dreaming of the world outside of Greenwood. But somewhere along the way, the world had swallowed them up.

Aditi had always been the glue that held the group together. She had kept in touch with everyone—sent messages, called, even arranged meetups though every time it felt as if something was slipping further and further from her grasp. They had grown apart, no matter how hard she tried to make things work. Still, when she had proposed this meeting, she had hoped that the old magic would return, that those childhood memories would come flooding back, and they'd fall right into place as they had so many years ago.

Aditi stood by the window of the familiar café, looking out at the bustling streets. She had arrived early, wanting to prepare for what felt like a pivotal moment. She glanced at her phone again, feeling a flutter of anxiety rise within her. Why hadn't Vikram responded? They had been in touch earlier in the week, confirming the details. So why was he late? And why hadn't he answered her messages?

Minutes passed, dragging with every second. When the door swung open, Aditi turned, hoping to see her friends. But instead, it was Rohit who entered first.

Aditi's heart dropped a little when she saw him. Rohit had always been the most carefree of the group, the one with the easy smile and the energy that could fill a room. But today, there was a noticeable weight in his eyes. His usual bright grin was missing, replaced by a tense frown, and he barely acknowledged her when he walked in.

"Aditi... Where's Vikram?" he asked, his voice low, almost flat.

"I... I don't know," she replied, forcing a smile. *"He should have been here by now."*

Rohit frowned and sank into the chair across from her, still not looking at her. His fingers twitched nervously, as if he didn't know where to put them. *"Something's off,"* he muttered to himself. *"I haven't heard from him either."*

Aditi's chest tightened. She couldn't shake the unease crawling under her skin. Why was he acting so distant? Something was clearly wrong, but she wasn't sure what it was.

Before she could ask another question, the door creaked open again, and this time, it was Arjun. The moment he entered, Aditi could sense the change in him too. The quiet, thoughtful guy she had once known had become someone else entirely. His eyes lacked their old spark, and his shoulders seemed weighed down by an invisible burden. He wasn't carrying his usual calm energy anymore. He looked tired both physically and emotionally.

"Where's Vikram?" Aditi asked as soon as he walked up to the table.

Arjun didn't greet her with his typical smile, nor did he sit immediately. He paused, staring out the window before speaking, his voice low and detached. *"He's not coming,"* he said flatly, his hands tucked into the pockets of his jacket.

"What do you mean he's not coming?" Aditi's frustration started to bubble up. *"We've been planning this for weeks. We all agreed. Why isn't he here?"*

Arjun sighed, rubbing his temples as if trying to stave off a headache. *"Because he doesn't want to be here."* His tone was colder than Aditi had ever heard it. *"And honestly, neither do I."*

Aditi blinked, her heart lurching. What had happened? The words felt like a slap to her face, and she couldn't understand why they were all so distant. She had imagined this moment for so long, and now that it was happening, it was nothing like she'd envisioned.

Rohit shifted uneasily in his chair, his eyes flicking between Aditi and Arjun. *"Okay, something's going on. What aren't you telling us?"*

Arjun stared at the table for a moment, avoiding both of their eyes. His voice dropped lower, almost to a whisper. *"Vikram doesn't want to fix anything. He doesn't think it's worth it anymore. We've all changed too much."*

"What? What do you mean?" Aditi's voice cracked as she asked the question. She felt as though the floor was slipping beneath her feet.

"He thinks it's too late," Arjun said slowly, his words heavy with bitterness. *"He says we're not the same people we were back then. That we've all grown apart, and the bond we had isn't even there anymore."*

Rohit shook his head vigorously. *"That's ridiculous. We've changed, yes, but that doesn't mean we can't still be friends. We've known each other since we were kids. If we can't fix this, then what the hell was all that time we spent together for?"*

Aditi felt the sting of those words. Rohit's frustration mirrored her own. She had been the one keeping in touch with everyone, trying to patch up the cracks, trying to hold on to the pieces of the past. But now, it seemed like it was all unraveling.

There was a long pause before Arjun spoke again. *"It's not just time. It's something else. Something I didn't want to say."*

Aditi's heart skipped a beat. She could sense that there was something darker lurking beneath the surface. She looked at Arjun, urging him with her eyes to continue.

Arjun exhaled slowly, his voice trembling slightly as he began to speak. *"There's something that happened a few years ago, during the camping trip. Vikram hasn't forgiven me for what I said."*

"What did you say?" Aditi asked, confused. She had been on that trip too, but she didn't understand what could have gone so wrong.

"I" Arjun paused, his face twisted with regret. *"I accused him of deliberately getting us lost. I was angry. We were cold, we were lost, and I needed someone to blame. But what I said to him... it broke something in him. He's carried that for years, and I've never properly apologized."*

The confession hit Aditi like a bolt of lightning. She stared at Arjun in disbelief. *He said that?* Vikram had always been the one to keep the group together during their more difficult moments. *For Arjun to have said that to him how could he?*

Rohit clenched his fists, his face turning red with anger. *"You said what?! Arjun, you accused him of sabotaging the trip? You know how important that was to him. You can't just drop something like that and expect it to be forgotten!"*

Arjun's face flushed with shame. *"I didn't mean it. I was just... frustrated. I've never forgiven myself for saying it."*

Aditi stood up, pacing. *"And you never told us this? You never told me?"* Her voice cracked, a mix of hurt and disbelief taking over.

"We should've talked about it. We should've fixed this a long time ago," Arjun muttered, his voice thick with emotion.

Rohit was silent for a long time, but when he finally spoke, his words were soft. *"Vikram is stubborn, you know that. But he's also hurting. He's never really been able to move past that, and he doesn't know how to forgive."*

"I never realized..." Aditi whispered. She felt as though the walls were closing in around her. Her thoughts swirled, tangled with all the things she'd never said, all the feelings she hadn't acknowledged.

They left the café and made their way to their childhood hideout, the old warehouse by the river. The setting sun was casting long shadows over the place, the air thick with the memories of their shared past. As they stood in the doorway, Aditi felt the weight of the years pressing down on her.

Rohit took a deep breath and turned to Arjun. *"If you really want to fix this, you need to apologize to Vikram. It's not going to be easy, but he's still your friend. He'll listen."*

Arjun nodded, looking at the ground. *"I will. I need to make it right."*

Aditi's heart fluttered with hope. Maybe it wasn't too late for them. Maybe, despite all the distance, despite the misunderstandings, there was still a chance to heal the wounds they had caused each other.

The rain started to fall softly, like a cleansing ritual over the years of silence. Together, they walked toward the future, uncertain of what would come next, but certain of one thing: the bond of friendship, though tested, could still be mended.

2
A Web of Betrayal

Priya sat in the dimly lit living room, her fingers nervously tapping the edge of the coffee table. She had spent days wrestling with the evidence proof of a betrayal that shattered everything she knew about her family. Her uncle, Ravi, had always been a pillar of support, a figure who had always seemed untouchable in her eyes. He had helped her father when the family business was struggling. He had promised to look out for her, to be her mentor. But now, that promise felt like a lie.

For the past few weeks, Priya had been digging into the company's financial records. It had started as a simple question why had the company's profits dropped significantly in the past year? But what she found went far beyond what she could have imagined. Ravi had been siphoning off funds, making shady deals with contractors, and forging signatures to cover his tracks. It was like a slap to her face she never thought her uncle, someone who had been like a father to her, could betray the family like this.

The revelation hit her hard, but the hardest part was what she had to do with it. Priya knew that exposing Ravi meant tearing apart the fabric of the family. But it was the right thing to do. She had to protect her family's legacy, even if it meant going up against the person she had trusted most.

It had been a week since Priya had uncovered the truth, and now the day had come. She sat in the living room, her mind racing. Her parents had no idea what she had discovered. They still believed in Ravi, still considered him an integral part of the family. Priya didn't know how they would react when the truth came out, but she knew one thing for sure her uncle's actions couldn't go unpunished.

Her phone buzzed, interrupting her thoughts. It was a message from Ravi, asking to meet her in the park. Priya's hands tightened around the phone as she read the message. He knew. He must have known she was onto him. This was it she couldn't delay anymore.

She stood up, her legs trembling. Priya had always been the quiet one, preferring to stay out of the limelight, but now, she had to be strong. For her family. For the truth.

The park was eerily quiet when Priya arrived. The wind rustled the leaves of the trees, and the scent of rain hung in the air. She saw Ravi sitting on a bench, his back turned to her. His familiar, warm smile was missing from his face. He looked... different. Tired. His shoulders slumped as if the weight of his secrets was finally catching up to him.

"*Ravi,*" Priya said, her voice steady but full of emotion. "*We need to talk.*"

He turned slowly, his eyes locking with hers. For a moment, they just stared at each other. The trust they once shared was gone, and now there was only a chasm of doubt between them.

"*I know what you're going to say, Priya,*" Ravi said quietly, his voice almost a whisper. "*You've found out everything, haven't you?*"

Priya's heart pounded in her chest. She didn't know if she was ready for this moment, but it had come. "*You've been stealing from us. From the family,*" she said, her voice breaking slightly.

Ravi didn't flinch. He didn't even look guilty. Instead, he sighed, as if the truth had already been revealed to him. "*I never wanted to hurt anyone, Priya. But sometimes you have to do what's necessary. The company was failing. Your father didn't see it, but I did. I had to make the hard choices.*"

Priya's eyes widened in disbelief. "*The hard choices? By lying, forging documents, stealing money from the company? That's not a choice, Ravi. That's betrayal. You've betrayed everyone.*"

He looked away, his jaw tightening. *"It wasn't supposed to be this way. I didn't mean for it to go this far."*

Priya stepped closer, the anger rising inside her. *"You took what wasn't yours, and you didn't even consider the damage it would do. To the business. To our family. To me."*

Ravi looked at her then, and for a brief moment, Priya saw a flicker of regret in his eyes. But it was gone in an instant, replaced by defiance.

"I've made mistakes, yes. But I did it because I thought I was saving us. It's too late now. What do you want me to do? Go back in time and undo everything?"

Priya's voice shook as she replied, *"You should have thought of that before you betrayed all of us. This is bigger than just you and me. You've hurt everyone."*

Ravi stood up, his expression hardening. *"I won't let you destroy everything I've worked for. Do you understand, Priya? I won't let you bring this family down."*

Priya stared at him, her thoughts racing. She had all the evidence, the proof that could ruin him. But even with that, she wasn't sure if she was ready for what would come next. Tearing the family apart, exposing the truth it wasn't something she took lightly. But it was the right thing to do.

That night, Priya didn't sleep. She couldn't. She sat at the kitchen table, staring at the evidence before her bank statements, contracts, emails. Everything she had uncovered. The truth was there, staring back at her. She knew what had to be done.

The next morning, Priya walked into the living room, where her parents were having breakfast. Her father looked up from his paper, smiling at her. Her mother was busy preparing a cup of tea. Everything seemed normal. But Priya knew it couldn't stay that way.

"Mom, Dad, I need to tell you something," she said, her voice firm. *"I've discovered something about Ravi..."*

Her parents exchanged a look, clearly concerned. Her father lowered the newspaper, and her mother stopped what she was doing, her expression turning serious.

"What is it, Priya?" her father asked, his voice laced with concern.

Priya hesitated for a moment before speaking, but there was no turning back now.

"Ravi has been stealing money from the company. He's been forging signatures and manipulating the accounts. I've gathered proof. Everything is here."

She handed them the evidence, her heart in her throat. Her parents' faces went pale as they read through the documents. The silence in the room felt deafening.

Her father's hands trembled as he set the papers down. *"I... I don't believe this. Ravi... he was like a brother to me."*

"I know it's hard to believe, but it's the truth," Priya said, her voice unwavering. *"We need to do something about it."*

Her mother's eyes filled with tears as she looked at Priya. *"What do you want us to do, Priya?"*

"We need to go to the authorities," Priya replied. *"We can't let this go on."*

The weeks that followed were filled with turmoil. The family business was in shambles, and the fallout from Ravi's betrayal shook the very foundation of everything Priya had known. Ravi tried to fight back, hiring expensive lawyers to cover up his actions. But in the end, the truth was undeniable. Ravi was arrested, and the family business was salvaged, though it would take years to rebuild the trust that had been broken.

As for Priya, she had won the battle, but it came at a great cost. The family was fractured. Her relationship with her parents was strained. She had torn open a wound that would never heal, no matter how much time passed.

But through it all, Priya knew one thing she had done what was right. The truth had come out, and justice had been served. And in the end, that was all that mattered.

3

Whispers of Loyalty

The rain poured down in heavy sheets, the kind that made the streets shimmer under the glow of the streetlights, and yet, Noah stood motionless, staring at the one spot where everything had changed. His dog, Max, sat by his side, as calm as always, looking up at him with eyes full of loyalty and trust.

Max was a **mixed-breed dog, his fur a patchwork of dark brown and black**, matted from the rain. His eyes, a striking shade of amber, held a depth that seemed to see more than just the world around him. He was larger than most dogs, with powerful legs that rippled with muscles, a lean yet imposing frame, and a calm, dignified demeanor. Despite his strength, there was an undeniable tenderness in the way he moved slow, purposeful, as if every action had meaning. His past was hidden in the lines of his fur, in the scars that marked his body, but his loyalty was unwavering. Max had always been Noah's protector, even when Noah didn't understand the depth of the bond they shared.

Noah, on the other hand, was a man in his **early thirties, tall, with broad shoulders** and a quiet intensity that made people take notice without him ever raising his voice. His dark brown hair was tousled from the rain, his face scruffy with a few days' worth of stubble. His deep-set eyes, the color of stormy skies, revealed the weight of the world on his shoulders, but there was also a flicker of hope in them a flicker that only Max seemed to be able to see.

His features were rugged, but kind, with a jawline that was slightly squared, giving him a determined, almost unyielding look. He was the type of man who carried his pain in silence, but Max had always known how to break through his walls.

Noah hadn't realized how much of his life had shifted when Max had entered it. It wasn't just the companionship, the quiet presence that made even the loneliest days bearable. Max had been there through the toughest times of Noah's life through heartbreak, failure, and moments when Noah had doubted his own worth. He had never asked for anything in return. He just loved. And in return, Noah had given him his heart.

But tonight, things were different.

"Come on, Max. Let's go home," Noah muttered, his voice barely rising above the sound of the rain. The storm had come out of nowhere, much like the phone call he'd received earlier that day the call that had shattered his world. **The call from his brother, Ethan.**

"Noah... Max is not just a dog."

Those words echoed in his head as he stepped forward, walking the path that would change everything. It was a secret, a truth that had been hidden from him for years. His brother's words had taken him to a dark place. He'd known for a while that something about Max's past was not quite right, but he'd never expected this.

"Max was part of a special program. He's not a stray. He was trained for something... much bigger."

The weight of Ethan's words felt like a heavy stone sinking deep in his chest. For years, Noah had believed that Max was just a regular dog his loyal companion who had come from a shelter, an animal that had found him when he needed him most.

But now, the truth had spilled over, and Noah's reality was breaking apart. Max wasn't just a dog. He had been trained as part of an underground program. An elite military operation. He had skills. He had been through training that Noah couldn't even begin to comprehend.

Noah remembered the night he had found Max at the shelter. The dog had been abandoned, neglected, a shadow of his former self. Yet, something about him had drawn Noah in immediately. Max had been different from the other dogs the way he moved, the way he watched people as if he understood them. He had been calm, but with an intensity in his eyes that made Noah question what he'd just adopted.

Noah had taken Max in without hesitation. The shelter worker had warned him, though. Max was a special case. A troubled dog, they had said. But Noah didn't care. He had needed something in his life to fill the emptiness, and Max seemed like the perfect fit. Over time, their bond had deepened. He had become Noah's best friend.

Max, however, never spoke about it. He just looked at Noah, always there, always protective. Always loyal. But now, with the truth unraveling before him, Noah was struggling to piece together the life he thought they had shared. He had trusted Max completely his best friend, the one who had never judged him, who had stayed by his side even when Noah had failed.

But now?

Noah's thoughts were interrupted as Max let out a low growl. He stopped, ears perked, his body tense. Noah's heart skipped a beat. Something was wrong.

"Max? What's..."

Before he could finish, a car screeched to a halt beside them, its headlights blinding him for a moment. The car door opened, and two figures stepped out. The first was a man, tall, with a hard expression etched into his face. The second, a woman, looked equally dangerous, with sharp, calculating eyes that assessed Noah instantly.

The man was built like a tank, his broad chest and arms giving him a commanding presence. His black hair was cropped short, and his dark, piercing eyes never left Noah's face. He wore a dark leather jacket, the kind of jacket that someone in his line of work would wear practical, worn, and tough. The man's face was rugged, with a permanent frown that spoke of years spent in high-stakes situations. His jaw was clenched, his fists balled at his sides, as if ready to take control of whatever situation came his way. Every move he made was calculated, a man who had seen too much and done things he could never take back.

The woman was equally as intimidating, her posture straight and commanding. She wore a tactical outfit, dark and fitted, that highlighted her athletic build. Her short-cropped blonde hair framed her face, and her eyes cold and calculating took in everything about Noah in one quick sweep. Her features were sharp, her movements swift, almost predatory. There was something unsettling about the way she looked at Max, as if she knew exactly what he was capable of.

"*Where is he?*" the man demanded. His voice was like gravel, rough and unyielding.

Noah's pulse quickened. "*Where's who?*"

"*The dog. Max. We know he's here.*" The woman's voice was smooth, but there was an unmistakable threat underneath.

Noah stood his ground, clutching Max's leash tighter. "*I don't know what you're talking about. Max is my dog.*"

The man's gaze flickered to Max, and something like recognition crossed his face. He took a step forward, but Max was ready. With a sharp bark, he lunged, his teeth showing in a warning snarl that made both strangers freeze.

Noah felt the hairs on the back of his neck stand up. He didn't know who these people were, but he knew one thing for sure these weren't ordinary strangers. Max's stance had shifted, defensive and alert, and Noah could see the years of training he had never known about now coming to the forefront. The dog he thought he knew was not the same one standing beside him now.

"*We don't have time for this,*" the woman snapped. "*Get out of the way, kid. This is bigger than you.*"

Noah's heart pounded in his chest. He had no idea what kind of past Max had, but one thing was clear his dog had been hiding it from him. And now, Noah was caught in the middle of something he didn't understand.

"*Max…*" Noah whispered, his voice trembling. He had never called the dog by his name like that before. It felt like a plea.

Max didn't move.

The woman stepped forward, but Max was faster. He lunged again, knocking her off balance, and in that moment, Noah understood. Max was not just a dog. He was a protector, and his loyalty went deeper than Noah had ever realized.

"No!" Noah shouted, rushing to Max's side. "Stop!"

The man pulled out a gun, but Noah was quicker. He grabbed Max's collar, yanking him back just as the gunshot rang out, missing them by inches. In that instant, Noah realized the depths of the danger they were in, and he was faced with a choice.

"Max, we need to go. We can't stay here," Noah said, his voice urgent.

The dog seemed to understand immediately. With a final look at the strangers, Max turned and bolted, Noah following closely behind, adrenaline pushing them both forward. They ran through the rain, through the alleyways, through the darkness, knowing they had no time to waste.

As they ran, Noah's thoughts swirled. Max had been part of something dangerous, something Noah had no idea about. But despite the betrayal, despite the shock, he realized that he couldn't just abandon Max now. He was more than just a dog. He was a friend, a protector, a silent warrior who had been guarding Noah for years.

By the time they reached the safety of their apartment, Noah was breathing heavily, his heart still racing. Max lay beside him, his eyes soft, but there was no sign of the dangerous creature he had just become moments before.

Noah sat down, running a hand through his damp hair. He looked at Max, and for the first time, he saw him for what he truly was not just a dog, but a guardian.

"What did you get me into, huh?" Noah said softly, his voice full of awe.

Max turned his head, looking at Noah with those intelligent, knowing eyes. And in that moment, Noah realized that whatever secrets Max held, whatever past he had been hiding, they were in this together now. The bond of loyalty, love, and trust was unbreakable, even in the face of danger.

Noah couldn't help but smile, knowing that, despite the storm that had torn through their lives, he would never be alone as long as Max was by his side.

4
The Signal Beyond

Dr. Nora Hunt stood in front of the towering console in the heart of the observatory. Her dark hair, tied back in a tight ponytail, framed her sharp features. Her gray eyes flickered across the monitor, scanning the data that had arrived in the early morning hours. Her fingers hovered over the keyboard, trembling with both anticipation and a creeping sense of unease.

"This doesn't make sense," she muttered to herself, leaning in closer, her voice barely above a whisper. She had been analyzing the signal for hours, the complex sequence of numbers repeating itself in a way that couldn't be natural. *"This is... no, it's impossible. It's a code. A message."*

Dr. Liam Clarke entered the room, his broad shoulders filling the doorway. His usual relaxed demeanor was gone, replaced with a tense energy. He had always been the calming presence in their partnership, but something in his eyes suggested that even he sensed the gravity of what was unfolding.

"What have you found?" Liam asked, stepping toward Nora, his voice low but filled with curiosity.

Nora didn't look up. She was too absorbed in her thoughts, her mind racing. *"A signal. From a star system that's supposed to be empty. But... this isn't random. There's an intelligence behind it. The frequency it's too precise, too calculated. And the timing... it's almost as if it's meant for us."*

Liam's brow furrowed. *"For us? What does that mean?"*

Nora hesitated for a moment before replying, her fingers hesitantly typing more data into the system. *"I don't know yet. But I'm going to find out. This could be the biggest breakthrough in human history."*

Liam crossed his arms, watching her. He had always admired Nora's brilliance, but today, there was something different. She seemed almost obsessed. He took a step closer, placing a hand gently on her shoulder. *"Nora, we've been through this before. Remember the last time you got this caught up in a theory?"*

Nora spun around, her gray eyes flashing with intensity. *"This is different, Liam. This is real. Do you hear it? The signal it's not just noise. It's a message, a warning, or something far greater than we understand."*

Liam sighed, running a hand through his tousled brown hair. *"Alright, I get it. But be careful, okay? You're diving headfirst into something that could change everything. And I don't want to see you lose yourself in it."*

She softened slightly, her gaze flickering to his face. *"I won't lose myself. But I need to know what this is. I need to understand."*

After several days of research and cross-checking the signal's origins, Nora and Liam managed to decode part of the message. What they found was both thrilling and terrifying: a set of coordinates that pointed to a remote research station in the Alaskan wilderness. The station had been abandoned, its data wiped clean, leaving only a chilling reminder of the project that had been halted in its tracks.

Liam looked at her, a mixture of worry and excitement in his eyes. *"You're really going to go there, aren't you?"*

"I have to," Nora replied firmly. *"This isn't just science anymore, Liam. This is something else. I feel it... in my bones."*

"I know," Liam murmured, his voice quieter than usual. *"But just... promise me you'll be careful. Whatever we're dealing with, we don't fully understand it."*

The station was as isolated as it was eerie. As they descended into the underground lab, the air grew colder, and the oppressive silence weighed heavily on them. The walls were lined with unfamiliar technology, broken and covered in dust. Yet, something about the place felt wrong, as if it had been abandoned in haste, but not without reason.

Nora approached the central console, her hands shaking as she powered it up. The screen flickered to life, showing encrypted files, old logs, and detailed blueprints of something unrecognizable. And then, in the center of the room, they saw it: a black, smooth object, nestled in the middle of a reinforced glass case.

Liam's voice was a whisper. *"What... what is that?"*

Nora stepped closer, her heart pounding in her chest. *"It's... it's the artifact. The one from the signal. This is what we've been searching for."*

She reached out to touch it, but Liam grabbed her arm, stopping her.

"No, Nora. Don't," he warned. *"We don't know what this thing is."*

"I have to," she insisted, shaking off his grip. *"This is the breakthrough. We can't just walk away from it."*

As her fingers made contact with the object, the world seemed to shift. The room grew darker, the air heavier. A low hum filled the space, and the artifact responded. It began to glow, first faintly, then brighter, until the entire room was bathed in a pulsating light.

Liam stumbled backward, his breath catching in his throat. *"Nora, what did you do?"*

Before she could answer, the hum stopped. There was an eerie silence, and then the air itself seemed to distort. And from the shadows, a figure stepped forward.

It was tall easily seven feet, its body slender and unnaturally pale. Its skin shimmered with an iridescent sheen, and its face was a blur of shifting shapes. But its eyes those eyes were infinite. They held the weight of galaxies, of time itself.

"I am Asar," the being said, its voice not heard, but felt in their minds. It was soothing, yet unsettling. *"I have come... from a future you will never see. I am the result of your choices, your evolution."*

Nora stood frozen, her mind racing to process the impossible reality before her. *"You... you're from the future?"*

"*Not from your future,*" Asar corrected, "*but from one of many. A version of humanity that transcended the physical. We were sent to warn you.*"

Liam stepped forward, his voice thick with disbelief. "*Warn us? Warn us about what?*"

Asar's expression was unreadable, but the sadness in its eyes was palpable. "*You are on the brink of destroying yourselves. The future you have built will collapse, and you will not survive the fall. But you*" Asar pointed at Nora, then Liam, "*have the power to change that. You must choose.*"

The world seemed to bend around them. A portal opened in the center of the room, swirling with unknown energy. Asar continued, "The future depends on the choices you make here and now. We are offering you the chance to undo the damage, but the cost will be high."

Nora looked at Liam, her eyes filled with uncertainty. "*What do we do? What's the right choice?*"

"*I don't know,*" Liam whispered, his voice thick with emotion. "*But whatever happens, we make it together.*"

Asar's gaze softened. "*Then the decision has already been made.*"

Hours later, when they returned to their lab, everything had changed. The artifact was gone. The coordinates no longer existed. The research station had vanished without a trace. They were left alone, with no memory of the decision they had made, but one thing was clear: the future had been altered.

As they stood outside, the sky above them was as still as a painting. The stars once distant and cold now seemed a little closer, a little more alive. Nora glanced at Liam, a sense of peace settling over her.

Liam turned to her, his face serious but soft. "*You remember?*"

She shook her head slowly. "*No. But I know we did something important.*"

He smiled, a flicker of hope in his eyes. "*Maybe that's enough.*"

And as the night stretched on, the universe seemed a little less lonely, as if the unknown had been slightly revealed.

5

The Last Diwali: A Magical Reconciliation

The city of Mumbai was alive with the spirit of Diwali the Festival of Lights. The air was filled with the sound of firecrackers, the smell of marigolds and sweets, and the chatter of neighbors lighting their diyas. But for Aisha, this year's Diwali felt empty. Her father, Anand, was gone, and the house they had once filled with laughter and joy now seemed hollow. She stared at the decorations the string of lights, the bright rangoli outside and felt her heart grow heavy. It was as if the house was trying to mask the absence of her father, but the silence was deafening.

Aisha walked to the window of the living room, gazing out at the city. The lights flickered in the distance, just like the memories of a time when everything had been perfect. She could almost hear her father's voice, calling her and her mother to come and join him for the Diwali celebrations. But now, it was just her and her mother, Suman, sitting in a house that was no longer a home.

"I miss him, too," Aisha whispered to herself, wiping a stray tear. But before she could retreat further into the shadows of grief, the doorbell rang.

Who could it be? Aisha wondered. She wasn't expecting anyone.

She opened the door slowly, only to find her estranged uncle Raghav standing there. The last time she saw him was over fifte years ago, after the bitter fallout with her father, Anand. Raghav had left the family, never once returning to make amends. But now, here he was, standing on their doorstep.

He was older, his face worn with time, but his eyes still carried the same weight of regret that Aisha remembered. His clothes were simple, and there was an almost apologetic aura about him. His presence was like a ghost from the past, a reminder of all the family secrets that had been buried.

"Aisha…" he began softly, his voice cracking as he stepped into the doorway. *"I know this isn't the right time, but… I need to speak with you. And with Suman."*

Aisha stood frozen, unable to say anything. The pain of years of abandonment, betrayal, and unspoken words rushed back. But there was something in Raghav's expression a vulnerability that made her step aside to let him in.

As Raghav walked through the door, his gaze lingered on the house. The vibrant lights, the rangoli, the smell of the sweets everything screamed of the family they used to be. But the laughter was gone. The warmth was gone.

"I know I'm the last person you want to see today," Raghav murmured, taking a deep breath. *"But I've come to make things right."*

Aisha crossed her arms. *"Make things right? After all these years, you think you can just waltz in and fix things?"*

Her words were sharp, but Raghav wasn't deterred. *"I know I don't deserve your forgiveness. I don't deserve your trust. But please, Aisha, let me explain."*

Before Aisha could respond, her mother, Suman, entered the room. Her face was pale, her hair unkempt, and her eyes lacked the sparkle they once had. She hadn't been herself since Anand passed away. The light in their home had dimmed, and Suman had retreated into her room, unable to cope with the void left behind by her husband's death.

Suman's eyes met Raghav's, and for a moment, time seemed to stand still. The years of hurt, betrayal, and silence hung between them like an invisible wall.

"*Aisha,*" Suman whispered, her voice breaking. "*Is he really here? After all these years?*"

Aisha, looking from her mother to her uncle, felt her anger intensify. "*He left us when we needed him the most, Mama. Why are you letting him back in?*"

Raghav stepped forward, his face etched with remorse. "*I was a fool, Suman. I've spent years regretting not being there when Anand needed me. When you needed me. I was wrong... so wrong.*"

Suman didn't say anything, but the tears began to fall. Raghav reached out for her, but she stepped back, her eyes full of pain.

"*I've waited too long for you to come back, Raghav,*" she whispered. "*Too long.*"

Then, unexpectedly, something strange happened. The lights flickered. The room became eerily cold. Aisha shivered, looking around the room as she felt a sudden shift in the air. The wind outside howled, and the sound of distant temple bells chimed as if something was calling them.

Raghav, who had been standing still, suddenly turned to face Aisha with an intensity she hadn't expected. "*There is something I have to show you,*" he said quietly.

Aisha was taken aback. "*What do you mean? What's going on?*"

Suddenly, the room shifted. The walls seemed to breathe, expanding and contracting like living things. The room grew dark, and Aisha felt the air thicken, pressing against her chest. Her heart raced in panic, and her breath caught in her throat.

"*What's happening?!*" she cried, looking desperately at her mother and uncle.

Before they could respond, a light began to form in the center of the room bright, radiant, and almost too intense to look at. It hovered in the air, casting strange shadows on the walls. Aisha felt an overwhelming pull toward the light, as though something was calling her from within.

Suddenly, the light exploded, and in its place stood a figure a glowing presence, humanoid in shape but not entirely human. Its skin shimmered with a strange, ethereal quality, and its eyes glowed with a deep, celestial blue. It hovered above the ground, its presence both comforting and unsettling.

Suman gasped, her hand over her mouth. *"What... what is this?"*

Raghav stepped forward, kneeling in front of the figure. *"I... I didn't want you to know like this. But the truth, Suman... Aisha... The truth about your father. Anand wasn't just a man. He was a guardian, a protector of ancient knowledge."*

The glowing figure nodded. *"Yes. Anand was part of a group of protectors who guarded the portal between worlds. The realm of light and the realm of darkness. He kept the balance, and when he died, the balance shifted. Now, Aisha, you must take his place."*

Aisha's mind spun, her thoughts a whirlwind. This can't be real. What is happening?

But the figure's voice was calm and soothing. *"You have the power within you, Aisha. The power to restore the balance. But you must choose to embrace it."*

Suman looked at Raghav, her face filled with shock. *"You knew about this? All these years, you knew?"*

Raghav nodded, his expression full of sorrow. *"I didn't want to burden you with it, but it's time for the truth to come out. We are all connected, Aisha. You have the bloodline of the guardians. Your father protected this world, but now, it's up to you."*

Aisha, still trembling, stepped forward. *"But I'm not ready. How can I...?"*

"You don't have to do it alone," the figure said gently. *"We will guide you. The light will always be with you."*

As the figure's glow faded, leaving the room in darkness once more, Aisha felt something deep inside her stir an awakening she couldn't explain. The truth about her father, the magic of the universe, and her own destiny was all intertwined in a way she could never have imagined.

The room, now calm again, felt warm as the lights returned. Aisha, for the first time in months, felt the weight of her grief lift. She looked at Raghav and her mother her family and knew that this Diwali, the Festival of Lights, would not only mark the end of a chapter but the beginning of something much greater.

"*I'm ready,*" Aisha whispered, her voice stronger than ever before.

Raghav smiled, his eyes filled with pride and relief. "*Together, we'll protect this world. Together, we'll heal.*"

As the family stood there, united in their newfound purpose, the lights of Diwali outside flickered brighter than ever, casting long shadows on the walls as the festival of light now more than just a tradition began a new chapter.

6
Festival of Hearts

The sun was setting over the small town of Varanasi, casting a warm golden hue over the streets. The city, known for its temples and ghats, came alive during the festival of Holi. The air was thick with excitement and anticipation. Children ran through the streets, their laughter echoing as they threw brightly colored powders into the air. The scent of freshly made gujiyas and thandai filled the air, inviting everyone to partake in the joyous festivities.

In a cozy house tucked away near the riverbank, the Verma family was preparing for the biggest celebration of the year. The house was filled with the sounds of music, the clattering of kitchenware, and the joyous chatter of family members getting ready for the evening.

Rajeev and Meera Verma, the parents, moved around their home with an infectious energy. They had been married for over two decades, and their love had only grown stronger with time. Their son, Arjun, a bright-eyed 18-year-old, helped his father string marigold garlands around the front door. His younger sister, little Anaya, giggled as she scattered rose petals on the floor, adding to the festive atmosphere.

As Rajeev looked at his family, a wave of gratitude washed over him. He had everything he ever wanted his beautiful wife, his two children, and a peaceful home filled with laughter. But as the day went on, there was something weighing heavily on his heart. His own father, who had passed away a few years ago, had always been the anchor of the family's Holi celebrations. This was the first year without him, and despite the cheerful atmosphere, Rajeev felt the absence deeply.

Sitting in the living room, Meera noticed the distant look in Rajeev's eyes. She knew him too well to not see that something was troubling him.

"Rajeev," she called softly, placing a hand on his shoulder. "*You're thinking about your father, aren't you?*"

Rajeev sighed, a bittersweet smile tugging at his lips. "Yes. *I miss him, Meera. Holi was always special because of him. He would tell stories, play with the kids, and make everything feel magical. I just... I don't know how to do that without him.*"

Meera sat beside him, her eyes filled with understanding. "*I know, Rajeev. I miss him too. But he lives on in our memories. And he would want us to celebrate, to be happy. Look at the kids. Arjun and Anaya are so excited for the evening. They don't even know how to mix the colors properly, but they're so eager to make everything perfect.*"

Rajeev glanced over at Arjun and Anaya, who were playfully arguing over which color should go into the bucket next. Anaya's bright laughter filled the air, and it was like the entire house came alive in response.

"*You're right, Meera,*" Rajeev said softly. "I should be grateful for what we have now."

The night fell, and the family gathered around the dinner table to share a meal before the celebrations began. The house was filled with the rich aroma of traditional dishes pulao, pakoras, and, of course, the much-anticipated sweets. As they sat together, the doorbell rang.

Arjun rushed to open the door, his face lighting up as he saw his cousins, the Sharma family, standing with arms full of colorful powders and sweets. They had traveled all the way from Lucknow to join the Vermas for Holi. The moment they stepped inside, the room erupted into hugs, laughter, and the joyous sounds of family reuniting.

"*Happy Holi!*" shouted Rajeev's sister, Nisha, as she hugged Meera. "*We wouldn't miss this for the world!*"

"*We're so happy to have you here,*" Meera replied, her voice thick with emotion. "*It's not the same without all of you.*"

The evening turned into a lively celebration. The children raced outside to play in the garden, tossing colors at each other, their laughter and shrieks filling the night air. Rajeev and Meera watched them from the porch, their hands intertwined.

"*You know,*" Meera said softly, "*I've been thinking about the first Holi we celebrated together. Just the two of us, before Arjun was born. It was so simple, so full of joy. I was so nervous having just moved to this city, not knowing anyone, but you made it feel like home.*"

Rajeev smiled at the memory. "*You looked so beautiful in that white saree. And you had no idea how to throw the colors properly, but you still tried, and I thought it was the sweetest thing.*"

Meera laughed, her eyes sparkling. "*I remember how you teased me for making a mess of it all. But we were so happy.*"

A long silence fell between them, filled only with the sounds of the children playing outside. Rajeev looked up at the sky, his heart heavy once more with the weight of the loss they had suffered. But then, as if on cue, he saw a shooting star streak across the sky. It was a sign, he knew it. His father was watching them, and he was smiling.

"*You know,*" Rajeev whispered, his voice thick with emotion, "I think Dad is here with us, Meera. I think he's right here in this moment. Watching the kids, seeing the family together again. It's exactly how he would want it."

Meera squeezed his hand, her eyes welling up with tears. "*I believe that too, Rajeev. I believe that he is with us, in every laugh, every color, every moment.*"

Arjun and Anaya ran up to them, their faces painted with vibrant hues of pink, green, and yellow. They were covered in powder from head to toe, their clothes stained with the colors of the festival. But their smiles, wide and uncontainable, filled Rajeev and Meera's hearts with a warmth that surpassed any words.

"Come on, Mama, Papa!" Arjun called excitedly. *"Come join us! The fun is just beginning!"*

Rajeev and Meera exchanged a glance, and without another word, they got up and joined their children. The whole family gathered in the garden, dancing to the beat of dholaks and laughing as the colors flew through the air. The night was alive with joy, with the celebration of life, and of memories, both old and new.

As they stood together, laughing and celebrating, Rajeev realized that this was the true essence of Holi not just the colors, the sweets, or the firecrackers, but the love and the togetherness that defined it. It was about honoring the past, celebrating the present, and knowing that the people we love are always with us, even when they are no longer physically here.

This Holi, they weren't just celebrating a festival they were celebrating family, love, and the beautiful memories that never fade.

And for the first time in a long while, Rajeev felt at peace.

7

The Boundaries Between

The sky was painted in shades of deep orange and violet as the sun dipped behind the towering mountains that surrounded the small town of Glenhaven. Nestled at the base of the mountains, the Deshmukh family had always lived a peaceful life quiet, secure, content. Or so they thought.

Ananya Deshmukh, a loving mother and wife, stood by the window in the kitchen, watching her son, Ishaan, play in the yard. He was young only 12 but already, there was something about him that felt... different. She couldn't quite put it into words, but she knew. And for some reason, as the days passed, she began to sense an undercurrent of unease.

"Mom, come look! The trees are glowing," Ishaan's voice rang through the air, high-pitched with excitement.

Ananya turned, her heart racing as she rushed to the window. The trees outside shimmered with an unearthly light, their leaves vibrating softly. She blinked. It couldn't be.

"Ishaan, what did you say?" she asked, her voice betraying a thread of unease.

But before she could get a clear answer, the door creaked open, and Arjun, her husband, entered. He was pale, his face tense. His eyes were wide with disbelief, his hands shaking.

"Arjun, what's wrong?" Ananya rushed to him, concern evident on her face.

"I think it's starting," Arjun murmured, barely above a whisper. *"It's real. All of it."*

"What's real?" Ananya's voice was tight with confusion. *"Arjun, what's happening?"*

"We've been living in a lie," he said, his voice cracking. *"Ever since we went to the cabin in the woods... I felt it. This this energy, this connection. I thought I was imagining it. But now... I know."*

"Energy?" Ananya shook her head. *"What are you talking about?"*

Before Arjun could answer, there was a knock at the door.

"I'll get it," Ananya said, her heart pounding. The air around her had begun to feel thick, almost suffocating.

She opened the door to find a tall, thin man standing in the doorway. His eyes glowed with an otherworldly hue bright, piercing, like they could see right through her. His expression was both calm and urgent.

"You're in danger," the man said, his voice low but firm. *"The boundaries are weakening."*

"I... I don't understand," Ananya stammered, but the man was already stepping inside, bypassing her as if he had been expected.

"I'm Kiran," he said, his voice clipped. *"I have come to warn you."*

"Warn us about what?" Arjun asked, his voice rising.

Kiran turned to face them both, his eyes scanning the room before speaking again. *"The fabric of this world and the next is thinning. And your son"* He paused, his gaze fixing on Ishaan, who was standing by the window, mesmerized by the glowing trees. *"Your son is the key."*

Ishaan, hearing his name, turned to face the stranger. *"What do you mean? Key to what?"*

Kiran moved closer, his eyes now filled with a strange intensity. *"You're linked to something ancient, Ishaan. Something bigger than both you and your family. Your bloodline is tied to the guardians of the realms. And the balance between those realms is about to break."*

Ishaan took a step back. *"No, I...I don't understand."*

"Listen," Kiran said urgently, *"I know this is overwhelming. But it's real. Everything you thought you knew, every law of physics you trust,*

it's nothing compared to what's about to happen."

Arjun shook his head, a bitter laugh escaping his lips. *"This sounds like a bad science fiction movie. Some kind of... portal to another world?"*

Kiran's expression remained stern. *"Not a movie. A reality."*

The room suddenly rumbled as if the ground itself was alive, and the windows shook in their frames. The air became charged, and a low, eerie hum filled the space.

Ananya stepped closer to Ishaan, her hands trembling. *"What's happening?"*

"The realms are colliding," Kiran said, turning toward the door. *"And unless you act now, everything will be consumed by chaos."*

Without waiting for a response, Kiran stepped into the yard. Ishaan, driven by a mix of fear and curiosity, followed him. The trees outside were glowing brighter now, pulsating like the heartbeat of something ancient. The air smelled of ozone, thick and heavy.

"We have to go," Kiran called over his shoulder. *"Time is running out."*

The family followed him into the woods, where the temperature seemed to drop drastically. A mist lingered just above the forest floor, twisting and moving like something alive.

As they approached the heart of the woods, an old cabin came into view. Weathered and worn, the cabin seemed to breathe with the forest itself.

"This is where it began," Kiran said. *"Your family is part of something much older than you realize. And Ishaan is the last of the guardians."*

Ishaan stepped forward, his heart racing as a sudden surge of power coursed through him. *"I don't feel like I'm anything special."*

"You are," Kiran replied. *"And now, you must open the portal before it's too late."*

At that moment, the sky above darkened, and a deep rumble sounded from the earth. It felt like the very fabric of space was warping.

"How do I open it?" Ishaan asked, panic in his voice.

Kiran handed him an old, intricately carved stone tablet. *"Place it in the center of the cabin. It will trigger the gateway."*

Ishaan hesitated but then placed the tablet on the floor. A bright light filled the room, and suddenly, the world seemed to twist. The walls of the cabin vanished, and they were standing on the edge of a vast, glowing realm a place filled with swirling energy and floating islands.

Ishaan gasped. *"Where... where are we?"*

"This is the other side," Kiran said. *"This is where the balance between the realms is kept."*

Suddenly, the light flickered, and dark clouds began to form, swirling into a massive storm that darkened the sky.

"This is what will happen if we don't act," Kiran said, his voice strained. *"The realms will collide and destroy everything. You're the only one who can stop it."*

Ishaan looked at his parents, who were now standing close together, their eyes filled with fear but also trust.

"I can do this," Ishaan whispered, feeling the weight of their gazes.

He turned to Kiran. *"What do I have to do?"*

Kiran gave him a grim smile. *"Unlock the power within you. It's always been there. You just need to accept it."*

The storm above them intensified, but Ishaan felt something inside him shift. A warmth. A power. He raised his hands, and suddenly, the energy around him responded. The light around the stone tablet grew brighter, and the storm above began to break apart.

"Do it, Ishaan!" Kiran shouted.

With a final surge of energy, Ishaan focused all his strength into the stone, and in that moment, the storm stopped. The realms settled. And for the first time in a long time, everything was calm.

The family stood together in the quiet, knowing they had just averted an unimaginable catastrophe.

But as they looked around at the serene landscape of the new realm, Kiran's voice broke the silence.

"This is only the beginning. The balance must be maintained. There will be more challenges. But you have proven that you are ready."

Ishaan turned to his parents, his voice soft but resolute. *"We'll face whatever comes together. We're a family, and nothing will break us."*

And with that, the family walked toward the horizon, ready for the new life that awaited them together.

8
The Echo of Love

Aria Matthews had always found solace in the world of music. From a young age, she had used it as a means to escape, especially after a childhood marked by foster homes and uncertainty. She was a petite woman with soft brown hair that cascaded just past her shoulders, her eyes a deep green that seemed to reflect every emotion she felt. Her voice was soulful, raw, and powerful, a reflection of everything she had lived through. Music was more than just her passion; it was her form of expression, the only language that had ever felt like home.

She lived in the bustling heart of San Francisco, performing at a cozy café that was known for its intimate ambiance and eclectic crowd. It was here, on one of those quiet evenings, that her world collided with Eliot Stevens. Or rather, someone who would soon become more than just a passing stranger.

Eliot was not just another face in the crowd. Tall and athletic, he carried himself with a relaxed confidence that commanded attention. His dark, tousled hair often fell into his piercing blue eyes, which were filled with both mystery and warmth. There was something inherently magnetic about him, and Aria couldn't help but be drawn to him the moment their eyes met during one of her performances. His gaze was steady, intense, as if he were trying to read every note that left her lips. In that brief moment, she felt a connection something deep and unspoken. He wasn't just listening to her music; he was feeling it with her.

After the performance, Eliot approached her. *"You were incredible,"* he said, his voice smooth and genuine. *"Your music... it feels like it's speaking to me. I haven't heard anything like it."*

Aria smiled shyly, sensing that there was something more to him than just an admiring listener. *"Thank you,"* she replied softly, feeling the warmth of his gaze linger on her. *"I guess music just pours out of me."*

Eliot's easy smile and the way he leaned in, genuinely interested in what she had to say, put her at ease. They exchanged stories, talked about their backgrounds, and bonded over shared experiences. He was an artist at heart as well, although he had never fully pursued his dreams. He worked as a graphic designer, but Aria could tell there was more to him than the professional façade he put on. He spoke of family, his love for art, and his longing to break free from the expectations placed upon him. Aria, despite her guarded nature, felt herself opening up to him in ways she hadn't done with anyone in years.

Days turned into weeks, and their bond deepened. Eliot, whose **real name was Alexander Duvall**, continued to be the perfect partner supportive, encouraging, and constantly reminding her to chase her dreams. He loved accompanying her to concerts, and whenever she felt insecure, his words of affirmation were a balm to her wounded heart. Aria, who had spent years building walls to protect herself from pain, was slowly letting them crumble. She had never felt this safe with anyone before, not even with her foster family. And for the first time in a long while, she believed that love could be something pure and real.

But as their relationship blossomed, Aria began to notice small inconsistencies. Eliot, despite being completely open about his life as an artist, never spoke of his family, and whenever the topic came up, he would skillfully change the subject. Aria, ever perceptive, couldn't shake the feeling that there was more to his past than he was letting on.

One afternoon, as they walked along the city's waterfront, Aria decided to confront him. *"Eliot, I mean, Alexander... I've been thinking. You never talk about your family. What's going on there? I feel like there's something you're hiding."*

His smile faltered for a moment, his eyes darting away as if searching for the right words. Finally, he took a deep breath. *"Aria, there's something I should've told you earlier. Something I've been running from for years. The truth is, I'm not just Eliot Stevens. I'm Alexander Duvall. I come from a wealthy family, and they've been pushing me to take over their business for years. It's not the life I want, but I've been too scared to break free."*

Aria felt her heart sink. The person she had let into her life, the person who had become her world, had been lying to her. *"But why? Why didn't you tell me?"* she whispered, her voice trembling with confusion and hurt.

"I didn't want you to see me as just another spoiled rich kid," he confessed, his voice raw with regret. *"I didn't want to lose you. Everything I've ever wanted is right here with you, Aria. But I was terrified that if you knew the truth, you'd leave me. I couldn't bear the thought of losing you."*

For a moment, Aria was silent, the weight of his words sinking in. She had spent her whole life being abandoned and hurt by people who didn't care about her, and now the person she loved had hidden a part of himself, unsure of how to trust her with the truth. The pain in her chest was overwhelming. *"I don't know if I can trust you now, Alexander,"* she said softly. *"I don't know who you really are anymore."*

"I understand if you need time," he replied, his voice barely above a whisper. *"I've been selfish, Aria, and I don't want to lose you, but I can't keep living this lie."*

The silence between them was suffocating, and just when it seemed as though their relationship might collapse under the weight of betrayal, Alexander's phone rang. He answered it, his face turning pale as he listened to the voice on the other end. The conversation was short, but it was enough to leave Aria feeling more confused than ever. He hung up and turned to her, his eyes filled with concern.

"Aria, I need to tell you something else. This is bigger than I thought. My family... they're involved in things I never expected. Dangerous things. And if you stay with me, you'll be dragged into it. I don't want that for you. I never did."

The revelation hit her like a storm. Not only had Alexander been hiding the truth about his identity, but now it seemed as though his family was tangled in a web of corruption, one that could destroy everything in their path. Aria, stunned and heartbroken, didn't know what to believe.

"I don't know what to do, Alexander," she whispered, tears streaming down her face. *"I love you, but I don't want to be a part of that world. I don't want to lose myself."*

"I'll do whatever it takes to keep you safe," he vowed. *"We can leave. We can run away from all of this. Together."*

And so they did. With nothing but their love and their dreams, Aria and Alexander escaped to a small town by the sea, far away from the reach of his powerful family. Over time, Alexander severed all ties with his past, cutting off his family's influence and choosing to build a life of his own. Aria's music flourished, her songs now carrying the weight of their shared journey. Their love, tested by secrets and danger, grew stronger with every passing day.

The small seaside town became their haven, a place where they could rebuild, not just their lives, but their trust in one another. Aria had always believed in the power of music to heal and express emotions, but now she knew that love, when it was real, could do the same. Together, they wrote their own story a story of redemption, resilience, and most of all, love that would never fade.

And so, in the quiet of their new life, with the sun setting over the ocean and their hearts beating in unison, they found peace.

9

Bound by Blood, United by Love

The rain had been falling relentlessly for days, casting a melancholic shadow over the small town of Evergreen. Inside a modest home, barely bigger than a cramped apartment, Sarah sat by the window, watching the droplets race down the glass. The old wooden shutters creaked in the wind, but the storm outside was nothing compared to the storm inside her heart.

Sarah Miller was a young woman in her mid-twenties. She had inherited her father's sharp, striking features: high cheekbones, a straight nose, and full lips. Her brown eyes, warm and determined, were the color of rich mahogany, radiating strength despite the exhaustion she carried in her heart. With long, brown hair that cascaded down her back in waves, she often tied it up in a messy ponytail when working around the house. Sarah was slim, and although her clothes were often plain due to their modest lifestyle, there was a quiet beauty about her that shone through even in her simplicity.

It had been three years since her **brother, Ethan,** left home to pursue his dreams in the city. Three years since the house had been quiet, with no sounds of his laughter, his spontaneous jokes, or the strumming of his guitar filling the rooms. Sarah never told anyone how much she missed him how the days felt colder, longer, and emptier without him.

Their family had always struggled financially. Their **father, Thomas Miller**, was a hardworking man in his mid-fifties, broad-shouldered with a thick, graying beard and steel-blue eyes. His hair had started to thin over the years, but his strong hands and weathered face were a reflection of his tireless work ethic. He always wore faded jeans and an old plaid shirt, looking like someone who had spent his entire life in a factory or construction site.

Their **mother, Linda Miller**, was a kind-hearted woman in her early fifties, with a soft face that seemed to glow with love. Her once-dark hair was now streaked with silver, usually tied up in a neat bun as she went about her cleaning work in the neighborhood. Her gentle brown eyes were always filled with warmth, and her smile could light up the darkest of rooms. Linda's strength was in her quiet grace, and she had an innate ability to make their cramped home feel like the safest place on earth.

Every time Sarah tried to carry on, she couldn't ignore the crushing weight of their circumstances. The house, once full of warmth, now felt too quiet, too small. She had to work multiple jobs to help her parents pay bills, her days filled with long hours of cleaning houses and washing dishes in restaurants. But no matter how tired she got, her heart remained steadfast. She knew her brother was out there, fighting his own battles, just like she was.

One rainy evening, the doorbell rang. Sarah jumped from her seat, heart racing, unsure of who would be visiting on such a dreary night. When she opened the door, her breath caught in her throat. Standing in front of her, soaked from the rain, was Ethan older, more mature, but unmistakably him.

Ethan Miller, at twenty-seven, had always been the charming, carefree sibling. He had the same sharp features as Sarah, but his face was softer, more boyish, with tousled dark brown hair that seemed to fall over his forehead in messy waves. His emerald green eyes, inherited from their mother, held a warmth that could make anyone feel safe. Ethan had always been lean and athletic, his tall, broad-shouldered frame now bearing the marks of a man who had lived through difficult experiences. His skin had grown slightly weathered from his time in the city, but there was still an undeniable glow to him. The faded denim jacket he wore clung to his frame, a contrast to the worn jeans and scuffed boots he had on.

"Ethan!" she gasped, her voice thick with emotion. Without saying another word, he pulled her into a tight embrace. The world outside faded as Sarah closed her eyes, savoring the feeling of being in his arms again.

"I'm home, sis," Ethan whispered, his voice low and shaky.

Tears welled up in Sarah's eyes as she pulled back, looking at him. *"You're really here,"* she whispered, as if she couldn't believe it.

Ethan smiled softly, brushing a strand of hair from her face. *"I should've come sooner."*

But Sarah could see the change in him the weariness in his eyes, the subtle tension in his shoulders. It was as if he had carried the weight of the world for too long.

Over the next few days, Ethan settled back into their modest home, though something was clearly different. He was quieter than before, sometimes staring out of the window for hours, as if lost in thought. Sarah could see it in the way he carried himself: a burden heavier than anything they had faced together before.

One night, Sarah could no longer stay silent. They were sitting at the small dining table, surrounded by a mound of unpaid bills and half-empty dishes, the flickering candlelight casting shadows on their faces.

"Ethan," Sarah said softly, *"What happened? What's going on?"*

Ethan's gaze dropped to the table, his fingers nervously picking at the edge of his plate. *"I messed up, Sarah. I thought I could make it on my own, that I could be successful in the city. But it was harder than I expected. I was too proud to admit that I needed help. And I... I couldn't make enough to send back home. I couldn't even pay for my own rent. I ended up in debt...and I lost everything."*

Sarah's heart ached as she reached across the table, her hand covering his. *"But you don't have to do this alone, Ethan. You have me.*

We've always had each other."

Ethan let out a bitter laugh, shaking his head. *"I've never been this lost. I thought I was doing it for us... for you. I thought I was going to come back and make it better. But I don't even know how to fix it now."*

Tears welled up in Sarah's eyes as she squeezed his hand. *"Ethan, we've faced worse. We grew up in a tiny house, with hardly any money, but we never gave up. We had each other, and that's what got us through. You don't have to carry everything on your own."*

Ethan looked at her, the sadness in his eyes evident. *"But I feel like I've failed you. You've always been there, always holding things together, and I wasn't there when you needed me the most. I should've stayed, Sarah. I should've never left."*

"Look at me," Sarah said, her voice unwavering. *"You didn't fail me. You're here now, and that's all that matters. We're family, Ethan. That's what we have each other. Nothing can take that away."*

The next few weeks were filled with late-night talks, deep conversations about their struggles, and the resilience they had learned from their parents. Ethan finally opened up about his time in the city: the loneliness, the financial struggles, the toxic relationships that drained him. He had tried to make it on his own, thinking that success and money would make everything better, but now he realized that the real success was in love, family, and community.

Sarah supported him through his struggles, even as they both worked harder than ever to pay bills and rebuild their lives. They didn't have much, but they had each other. Slowly, Ethan began to regain his confidence. He started studying for the **Chartered Accountancy (CA) exams** again, a dream he had put on hold for so long. After everything that had happened, he knew that this was his chance to rise up from the ashes, to fulfill his dreams, and to make his family proud.

Late one night, after months of grueling work, Ethan looked up from his textbooks, the light from the lamp casting a soft glow on his tired face. *"Sarah,"* he said, his voice full of determination, *"I've got one last shot. I'm sitting for the final CA exam next week."*

Sarah smiled, feeling a sense of pride swell in her chest. *"You've got this, Ethan. I know you do."*

Weeks later, the results were released. Sarah was the first to see them, her hands trembling as she opened the email. The world seemed to slow down as her eyes scanned the message.

Ethan had passed the CA exam.

She could hardly believe it. She ran into the living room, holding her phone high. *"Ethan! You did it! You passed! You're a Chartered Accountant!"*

Ethan stood still for a moment, his eyes wide with disbelief. Then, slowly, a smile spread across his face. *"I did it... I really did it."*

The following months were filled with interviews, tense moments, and a few setbacks. But then, one day, Ethan received a call that changed everything. A prestigious multinational company had offered him a position one that promised a future full of opportunities, success, and stability.

When Ethan shared the news with Sarah, her face lit up. *"This is it, Ethan. You did it. You worked so hard, and now it's paying off."*

Ethan looked at her, his voice full of gratitude. *"I never could've done this without you, Sarah. You were always there, even when I thought I couldn't make it. You never gave up on me."*

And in that moment, Sarah realized that no matter how poor they had been, no matter how many obstacles they faced, they had always been rich in love, in dreams, and in the unwavering support they gave each other.

Together, they had overcome the most difficult years of their lives, and now, with Ethan's success, they had a new beginning ahead of them a life filled with possibilities, driven by the love they shared and the dreams they had fought so hard to make a reality.

As the rain finally stopped, they sat together on the porch, the night filled with stars, knowing that they had faced the storm and come out stronger, side by side, bound by blood, united by dreams.

10

The Lost City of Astralan

The jungle pressed in on them like an impenetrable wall. The air was thick with humidity, the dense vegetation curling and twisting around them as though it had a life of its own. The only sounds were the distant calls of unseen creatures and the rustling of leaves as Alex and Isla navigated through the jungle, their clothes damp from sweat, their bodies aching from the exhausting trek. They had barely spoken in the last few hours, each lost in their own thoughts, but the tension between them was palpable.

Alex Donovan, a seasoned explorer in his mid-thirties, had a rugged charm about him. His brown hair, a little too long and wind-tousled, framed his sharp jawline, and his dark, hazel eyes held a depth that revealed years of experience in the field. He was strong and practical, yet there was a warmth to him, a side that only those closest to him could see. Though his confident exterior rarely wavered, deep down, Alex carried the weight of the many mysteries he had uncovered and the few that had remained unsolved.

Beside him, **Isla Carter** was a contrast to his hard-edged demeanor. A younger woman in her late twenties, Isla was curious and thoughtful, with wide green eyes that always seemed to be absorbing everything around her. Her blonde hair was tied back in a messy ponytail, strands falling free from the heat. There was something graceful in the way she moved through the jungle, as if she belonged to this wild world. A talented archaeologist, Isla's fascination with ancient civilizations had brought her to Astralan with Alex. But as much as she loved history and uncovering lost truths, she couldn't deny that part of her had hoped to leave the city's mysteries untouched.

Isla paused for a moment, wiping the sweat from her forehead, and looked at Alex. *"I'm not sure how we made it out of there alive,"* she said, her voice filled with a mix of exhaustion and disbelief. *"That orb... it changed everything."*

Alex looked back at her, his jaw clenched in thought. *"I don't know how it happened, but I'm not ready to leave without understanding what we found. There's something important about that city, Isla. Something that's pulling us back."*

Her brow furrowed as she cast her gaze down at the map she had carried all this time now frayed and torn from the journey. *"We need to be careful,"* she said quietly, more to herself than to him. *"There's more to this place than we realize. More danger. I don't trust what happened back there."*

The two of them continued on, their boots sinking into the soft earth beneath the thick layers of vegetation. The sun was beginning to set, casting long shadows over their path. The oppressive heat of the jungle seemed to have grown more intense as the light faded. And that's when Alex stopped, his body tense, his eyes scanning the surroundings. He held up a hand to signal Isla to stop.

"Do you hear that?" he whispered.

Isla's heart skipped a beat. She strained to listen but heard nothing at first. It was then that a soft rustle broke the eerie stillness around them, a sound that sent a chill up her spine. Someone or something was moving in the underbrush, and the sound was growing closer.

"Alex," Isla whispered, her voice barely audible. *"We're not alone."*

Alex nodded, pulling the machete from his waist as his eyes narrowed. His gaze flickered to the shadows of the trees around them. *"Stay close."*

Moments later, a figure emerged from the darkness between the trees a man, disheveled and gaunt, his clothes torn and stained with dirt. His eyes were wide with panic, his face thin and drawn. His voice, when he spoke, was barely a whisper, hoarse and strained. *"You shouldn't have come back."*

Isla recoiled slightly, instinctively moving closer to Alex. *"Who are you?"* she demanded, her voice shaky but defiant.

The man's face was wild with something between fear and madness. His skin was pale, and the dark bags under his eyes suggested that he had been living in the jungle for far too long. *"I was like you,"* he rasped. *"Curious. Searching for the city's secrets. But you don't know what you're dealing with. The city..."* His voice faltered, his eyes darting to the jungle around them. *"It's cursed. Once it has you, it doesn't let you leave. You will never escape."*

Alex stepped forward, his gaze hardening. *"What are you talking about? Who are you? What happened to you?"*

The man's gaze locked onto Alex's, and for a moment, it was like a flicker of recognition passed between them. Then, with a guttural groan, the man staggered back and collapsed to the ground. His body went still, as though some invisible force had drained the life from him.

Isla gasped and took a step back, her hand covering her mouth. *"What just happened? Did he die?"*

Alex knelt beside him, checking for a pulse. There was nothing. *"He didn't die naturally,"* Alex muttered, standing up and looking around. *"We need to move. This place... it's dangerous."*

They didn't need to say anything else. Without a word, they continued on their way, the darkness of the jungle closing in around them. But even as they walked, neither of them could shake the man's warning from their minds.

Night had fully descended when they finally found the river. It was a relief to see the water, its soft rushing sound a welcome contrast to the haunting stillness of the jungle. The river had been their guide into the city, and it would be their guide out.

Alex and Isla paused for a moment, standing at the edge of the water, both feeling the weight of the journey pressing on their shoulders.

"We're not out of danger yet," Alex said, looking at Isla. "But this is the right way."

Isla nodded but couldn't shake the memory of the man's words. *"Do you think it's true? What he said about the curse?"*

"I don't know," Alex admitted. *"But I'm not leaving without answers."*

The two of them crossed the river, their footsteps cautious but sure. As they moved along the banks, the forest seemed to shift and whisper around them, the shadows playing tricks on their tired minds. Their eyes scanned every movement, every sound.

They finally reached the village, where the quiet villagers greeted them cautiously. The village was humble, but the people were welcoming. One villager, an older man with a weathered face, approached them.

"You two have been in Astralan, haven't you?" he asked, his voice tinged with awe and fear.

Isla and Alex exchanged glances before nodding. *"Yes, but we need to know more,"* Alex said. *"What's the truth about Astralan?"*

The old man sighed deeply and looked around as if checking that no one else was listening. *"The truth about Astralan is that it was never meant to be found. The city's magic, its power it pulls people in and never lets them go. You two are the lucky ones. Most never return."*

Alex and Isla looked at each other, their minds filled with more questions than answers. But for now, they had escaped the jungle alive, and that was enough.

However, as they turned their backs on the village and walked away, the looming silhouette of Astralan seemed to follow them, its mysteries still waiting. The city hadn't finished with them yet.

They had only just begun.

11

The Kingdom of Aranyara

In the heart of the lush, untamed wilderness of Aranyara, a diverse community of animals had lived in harmony for generations. The trees stretched high, the rivers ran clear, and the air was filled with the sounds of life. However, all of that was about to change. An unrelenting force was closing in on their world the destructive hands of human greed.

Luna, the wise lioness who had long protected her kingdom, watched with sorrow as the horizon grew ever more tainted. The once-beautiful landscape had been marred by machines that bulldozed through their forest, tearing apart the homes of many animals. The air had grown thick with dust, and the river once a source of life was now polluted with toxins.

Luna's golden fur shimmered under the sun, her amber eyes reflecting the pain of a land slipping into ruin. She was the leader, the one who had always held the kingdom together. But now, there was an overwhelming sense of helplessness in the air.

"We cannot stand by any longer," Luna said, her voice carrying the weight of generations. *"The humans have gone too far. Our home is disappearing before our eyes."*

Beside her stood Kavi, the towering elephant whose massive presence commanded attention. His tusks gleamed in the fading light, but the sorrow in his eyes mirrored Luna's. *"It's not just the forest. The wildlife is disappearing. We need to find a way to stop this before it's too late."*

"*How?*" asked Finn, the small rabbit who had always been quick on his feet but slow to act. His fur twitched with anxiety. "*Humans are too powerful. What can we do against them?*"

Grimm, the grizzly bear with a heart of gold and paws that could crush boulders, shook his massive head. "*The problem is bigger than us. It's the loss of our homes, the loss of our food sources, the loss of our sanctuary... we are being pushed to the brink. But we cannot lose hope."*

Lyra, the graceful dove, fluttered in beside the group, her wings beating softly against the quieting air. "*We need a plan. We need to protect the last sanctuary we have left. The human forces are closing in, but they haven't found the Heart of the Forest yet. If we can get there, we can protect it."*

Luna nodded. "*The Heart of the Forest... it's said to be where the land is most sacred, the place where the magic of our world is still strong. If we can keep it hidden, the humans won't be able to destroy everything."*

The group made their way deeper into the forest, through the parts that were still untouched, where the trees stood tall and the sounds of nature flourished. Along the way, they encountered more signs of destruction cleared land where forests used to stand, burned areas where animals had once roamed freely. The devastation was everywhere, and it felt like time was running out.

As they neared the Heart of the Forest, a place hidden from human eyes, they encountered a formidable problem. Poachers humans who hunted animals for sport had set up traps, and they were not just after the wildlife. They were after the Heart itself, intending to strip the forest of its life force for profit.

"*We can't let them find it,*" said Luna, her voice tinged with fear. "*The Heart is the last hope for all of us. If they take it, everything will be lost."*

Kavi stepped forward, his voice powerful and commanding. "*We cannot let them destroy the last piece of what makes this land sacred. We will fight for it, with everything we have."*

But Finn, the nervous rabbit, was unsure. "*We're too few. They have weapons, traps, and tools we can't fight with. How can we stand against them?"*

Grimm, his deep voice steady, spoke up. *"It's not about fighting. It's about outsmarting them. We know the land better than they do. We know the hidden paths, the caves, the secret places. We will lead them away from the Heart, confuse them, and buy ourselves time."*

The group began their strategy. They worked together each animal using their unique abilities to set traps for the poachers, to mislead them into dangerous territories, and to cover their tracks. Lyra, with her keen sense of direction, flew high above, keeping watch on the poachers' movements. Kavi used his massive size to create obstacles, blocking roads and paths where the poachers might come. Grimm's knowledge of the forest allowed him to identify the safest routes to take.

But just as they were about to reach the Heart of the Forest, disaster struck. The poachers had set up a perimeter around it, catching the group off guard. Their final stand was about to take place.

Luna looked at her friends, determination shining in her eyes. *"This is it. We cannot run. We fight for the future of Aranyara. We fight for our home."*

The group charged forward. Kavi led the way, using his tusks to charge through the poachers' barricades. Finn darted in and out of the shadows, leading the poachers into traps. Lyra swooped down, distracting the enemies with swift maneuvers, while Grimm charged in to protect them. Rex, who had joined the group despite his past mistakes, used his agility and strength to flank the poachers from behind.

The battle was fierce, but the unity of the animals shone through. Each member of the group played their part, pushing the poachers back. In the end, it wasn't their strength that won the fight; it was their unity, their courage, and their love for their home.

As the poachers were forced to retreat, Luna stood in the Heart of the Forest, her head held high. The danger was over for now. The forest was safe.

The animals gathered around Luna, the weight of their victory settling in. They had fought not just for their own survival, but for the survival of the entire ecosystem. The forest, the river, the creatures everything was interconnected, and their victory ensured that harmony would continue for generations to come.

Finn looked up at the others, a smile creeping across his face. "*I didn't think we could do it, but we did. We saved the Heart.*"

Kavi's deep voice rumbled with pride. "*We didn't just save the Heart. We saved our home. Together.*"

Grimm nodded in agreement. "*When we work as one, nothing can defeat us.*"

Rex, who had once felt like an outsider, finally felt a sense of belonging. "*I may have lost my way before, but today... today, I fought for something worth believing in.*"

Luna looked around at her friends her family. "*This is just the beginning. The fight to protect our world never ends. But together, we'll always find a way.*"

The animals returned to the heart of their kingdom, where the forest began to heal, the rivers ran clear again, and the wildlife slowly returned. The battle was not over, but the fight for Aranyara was one they would continue to face together stronger, braver, and united in the love for their home.

And so, the animals of Aranyara stood together, not just to protect the forest, but to ensure the survival of all that they held dear.

12

The Silent Echo

In the neon-lit streets of Vienna, where shadows cast long and secrets whispered through the alleys, a man named **Maximilian Drake** *lived a life few could ever imagine. Tall, dark-haired, with an aura of mystery about him, Maximilian was no ordinary man.* His piercing green eyes held secrets that had been buried deep for years, secrets that only a handful of people in the world could truly understand.

Maximilian was a spy.

Not the kind that you see in the movies, with tuxedos and fast cars, though he was skilled with a gun and knew how to handle himself in a fight. No, Maximilian was part of an underground network a secret government agency so discreet that it operated in the gray area of international law. Their missions were often too dangerous, too sensitive for the public to know. Their job was simple: protect the world from the shadows, even if it meant becoming a shadow themselves.

But lately, things had become complicated. A cryptic message had come across Maximilian's desk, a simple line that read: ***The Silent Echo is real.***

He knew that code. It was a phrase used by an elusive *criminal syndicate known as The Acheron Group.* For years, they had evaded capture, leaving behind nothing but death and destruction in their wake. They were ghost-like no trace of their existence, no clear motive, just a trail of chaos wherever they went.

Maximilian's mind raced as he sat in his office, staring at the message. He had dealt with them before, but this was different. The Silent Echo was a project a weapon rumored to have been developed in secret. But no one knew exactly what it was or who was behind it. Maximilian was assigned to find out. His first clue led him to a woman named Adelaide Rivers.

Adelaide was a detective, but not like any detective Maximilian had met. She was sharp, calculating, and she had a reputation for solving cases that seemed impossible. She had been tracking the Acheron Group for years, but unlike Maximilian, she wasn't part of any secret agency. She was just a woman with a relentless desire for justice.

Maximilian's mission was clear: work with Adelaide, find out what The Silent Echo was, and stop the Acheron Group before they could unleash whatever dangerous weapon they were planning. But there was a problem. Adelaide wasn't just a skilled detective she had a past, one that seemed tied to Maximilian's own.

The first meeting was in an abandoned warehouse on the outskirts of the city. The dim light filtered through the cracks in the walls, casting long shadows that made it hard to see who was friend or foe. Adelaide stood near the entrance, her silhouette sharp against the dim light. She wore a leather jacket, her long dark hair tied in a ponytail, and her eyes were scanning the area with practiced vigilance.

"Maximilian Drake," she said when she saw him, her voice steady, but her eyes unreadable.

"Adelaide Rivers," Maximilian replied, his tone equally guarded. *"You've been a hard person to find."*

"And you've been harder to trust," she said with a slight smirk, folding her arms. *"But here we are."*

Maximilian studied her closely. There was something about her, something he couldn't put his finger on. She wasn't just a detective. There was a fire in her eyes, a deep sense of purpose that spoke to him.

"Look, we don't have much time," Maximilian said, his voice taking on a more serious tone. *"The Acheron Group is planning something. The Silent Echo is more than just a rumor. It's real. And we need to find out what it is, before it's too late."*

Adelaide's eyes darkened at the mention of the Acheron Group. *"I've been following their trail for years, but they're ghosts. They cover their tracks well."*

"We've both been chasing shadows," Maximilian admitted. *"But this time, we're going to catch them."*

As the two of them ventured deeper into the underworld of Vienna, their paths collided in unexpected ways. They discovered that the Acheron Group had infiltrated high levels of government and corporate industries, weaving a tangled web of power and influence. Their influence reached every corner of the city, and finding the truth meant pulling at threads that could unravel everything they thought they knew.

The deeper they dug, the more the two of them began to rely on each other. Adelaide's detective work, combined with Maximilian's spy training, made them a formidable team. But they both carried scars from the past scars that were tied to the Acheron Group.

One night, as they followed a lead to a hidden lab beneath an old hospital, they stumbled upon a horrifying discovery. A woman, bound to a chair, with wires attached to her head. Her body was frail, her skin pale. But her eyes those eyes were familiar to Maximilian.

"Is it her?" Adelaide whispered, her voice a mix of disbelief and horror.

Maximilian felt his heart drop into his stomach. The woman in the chair was Lena, his sister, who had disappeared without a trace years ago. Maximilian had always assumed she was dead, another casualty of the shadowy world he lived in. But there she was, alive, her mind shattered by what had been done to her.

Lena's eyes flickered open as they approached. She didn't speak, but her eyes locked onto Maximilian's, and in them, he saw a deep, haunting recognition. The silence between them was thick with unspoken words.

"*Lena,*" Maximilian whispered, his voice breaking. He reached out, but before he could touch her, alarms blared, and the entire facility began to shake.

"It's a trap," Adelaide yelled, pulling Maximilian away. "*We need to move, now!*"

But it was too late. The doors slammed shut, and armed guards poured into the room. Maximilian and Adelaide fought fiercely, their every move calculated and precise. But it was clear that they were outnumbered. Just as they were about to be overwhelmed, a voice crackled over the intercom.

"*You've come too far, Maximilian,*" the voice said coldly. "*The Silent Echo is already in motion. It's already too late.*"

Maximilian's heart raced. This was it. The mission he had been assigned to was no longer about uncovering secrets. It was a race against time. The Acheron Group was about to unleash their weapon, and he had no idea what it could do.

With Adelaide by his side, Maximilian managed to escape, but Lena's fate remained uncertain. They couldn't afford to go back for her not yet. They needed to stop the Acheron Group before the weapon was activated.

The final showdown took place at an underground facility hidden deep beneath the city. The Acheron Group's leader, a man known only as The Director, stood in front of a massive control panel, ready to unleash the weapon. Maximilian and Adelaide infiltrated the facility, their movements swift and silent. But as they approached, a shocking twist awaited them.

The Director wasn't just some criminal mastermind. It was Maximilian's father, a man who had faked his death years ago, manipulating both sides of the world for his own gain.

"*You should've stayed out of this, Maximilian,*" his father said coldly, staring down at his son with a mix of disdain and disappointment. "*This is bigger than you can understand.*"

Maximilian's world shattered. His father, the man who had disappeared, had been pulling the strings all along.

In the final, tense moments, with the weapon's countdown ticking down, Maximilian had to make a choice save his father, or save the world.

He made the hardest decision of his life. With Adelaide's help, they destroyed the weapon, ending the Acheron Group's reign. As the facility crumbled around them, Maximilian's father tried to escape but was caught in the blast. He died with no one to mourn him but himself.

In the aftermath, Lena was rescued, though she would never fully recover from the trauma. Maximilian and Adelaide, forever changed by the mission, walked away from the wreckage. They didn't speak of their past, but they both knew their lives would never be the same.

And so, as the sun set over Vienna, the Silent Echo that had haunted them all was finally silenced.

13

When Love Fades

The city had always been a maze of faces and voices, each one blending into the next, indistinguishable from one another. But for Ivy, there was always a sense of clarity about her life, until she met Noah.

Ivy had spent years living a quiet, somewhat monotonous life. **A successful but reserved architect**, Ivy kept her life focused on her career. She didn't have time for distractions especially love. Her life was built on solid, carefully designed plans and structures, her days filled with meetings, deadlines, and endless paperwork. But deep down, she longed for something more something real.

One rainy evening, Ivy decided to take a walk to clear her mind. As she strolled through the narrow streets of the city, her thoughts were heavy. The sound of her heels clicking on the pavement was the only thing breaking the silence around her. That's when she collided with him. She hadn't seen him coming, and before she knew it, she was sprawled on the wet ground.

"Are you okay?" a deep, concerned voice asked, accompanied by a warm hand reaching out to help her up.

Looking up, Ivy met the eyes of Noah, a man who exuded an undeniable charm. He had messy dark hair, a casual, almost disheveled appearance, yet there was something captivating about his presence. His eyes were intense, full of life, yet there was a touch of sadness behind them, something that made Ivy feel both drawn to and wary of him.

"I'm fine, just not paying attention," Ivy replied, brushing herself off. She stood up, trying to hide the small blush creeping up her neck from the awkward encounter.

Noah chuckled. *"I should have looked where I was going. Let me make it up to you. Coffee? My treat."*

Ivy hesitated, the urge to decline gnawing at her. But for reasons she couldn't explain, she found herself saying yes. They walked to a nearby café, and Noah ordered two lattes. They sat by the window, watching the rain pour down, and for the first time in a long while, Ivy felt at ease.

Their conversation flowed easily, as if they had known each other forever. They talked about their lives, their childhoods, their passions. Noah revealed that he was a struggling musician, trying to make it big in the city, while Ivy spoke about her work as an architect and her dreams of designing something truly monumental.

As the hours passed, Ivy felt a connection she hadn't felt in years. She wasn't sure what it was his gentle charm, the way he seemed to understand her more than anyone had but she felt something stirring inside her. Maybe it was time for a change.

Weeks went by, and Ivy found herself looking forward to their late-night walks, dinners in small restaurants, and long conversations. She started seeing a side of Noah that was rare he was broken, yet hopeful; lost, yet determined. Every time they spoke, he seemed to get closer to her. He showed her his music, played his guitar for her under the stars, his voice low and soothing. He opened up about his struggles: growing up in a broken home, his failed relationships, his constant fight to make his passion his career. And Ivy, ever the observer, was moved. It felt like Noah was the missing piece she never knew she was searching for.

They became inseparable, and Ivy, for the first time, felt her walls breaking down. She began to allow herself to be vulnerable with him, telling him about the pain she had buried for years the pressure of success, the loneliness that came with her career, the fear of failure that haunted her at every turn. Noah listened, never judging, always encouraging. He made her feel like she could breathe again.

But as their connection deepened, something began to change in Noah. He started pulling away. It was subtle at first he was always late, his messages became infrequent, his mood more distant. Ivy, always so aware of her surroundings, noticed the shift. She confronted him, but Noah always had an excuse. *"I'm just busy with work, Ivy. I'll be better, I promise."*

But Ivy's instincts told her something was wrong. She couldn't put her finger on it, but she felt it a sense of impending doom. The love they shared, so vibrant and alive, now seemed tainted by the unspoken distance growing between them.

One evening, Ivy waited for Noah at their usual café. She had prepared herself for a conversation she had been avoiding one where she needed to ask the tough questions, the ones that had been gnawing at her. She needed the truth.

Noah arrived late, as always, but this time there was something different about him. His eyes were bloodshot, his face pale, as if he had been awake for days.

"Ivy," he started, his voice cracking slightly. *"I need to tell you something."*

Ivy felt her stomach drop. The air around her seemed to grow thick with tension. She nodded, her pulse quickening.

"I'm not the person you think I am," Noah continued, his eyes filled with regret. *"Everything about me has been a lie."*

Ivy's heart pounded in her chest. *"What do you mean? What are you talking about?"*

"I've been using you, Ivy. All this time. My music? It's just a front. I'm in debt. Deep debt. And I've been running from it, trying to keep up the illusion of being this carefree musician. But it's all falling apart. I've been hiding from the truth, hiding from the people I owe. And now they're threatening me."

Ivy sat in stunned silence, the weight of his words sinking in. She couldn't believe what she was hearing. The man she had come to love, the one she had trusted with her heart, had been hiding a world of lies.

"I'm so sorry, Ivy," Noah whispered, his voice breaking. *"I never meant to hurt you. But I don't know how to fix this."*

Tears welled up in Ivy's eyes as she processed the betrayal. The man she had believed in, the man she thought was her soulmate, had been lying to her from the beginning.

"No," Ivy whispered, shaking her head. *"No, you don't get to do this. You don't get to destroy everything we built."*

"Ivy, please," Noah begged, reaching out to her. *"I never wanted this. I never wanted to hurt you."*

But it was too late. The illusion was shattered, and Ivy's heart was broken. The love she thought they had was a lie, a carefully constructed façade. She stood up, tears streaming down her face, and walked out of the café without looking back.

That night, Ivy didn't sleep. She cried for the love she had lost, for the trust that had been broken. But in the midst of the heartbreak, she knew one thing: she was stronger than she had ever been before. And no matter how much Noah had hurt her, she would rebuild. She would find her way back to herself.

And as for Noah? He had made his choice, and now, he would have to live with the consequences.

14
Unbreakable Will

In a small town nestled between hills, there was a **group of five girls** whose lives were intertwined by fate. Each of them came from different backgrounds, each with unique dreams, struggles, and aspirations, but together they formed an unbreakable bond that allowed them to overcome everything life threw at them.

The leader of the group was **_Zara, a tall, fiery young woman_** with a sharp mind and a passion for justice. Her jet-black hair cascaded down her back, and her piercing green eyes held a fire that could make anyone think twice before underestimating her. Zara came from a broken family, raised by her single mother after her father had abandoned them. From an early age, Zara had learned to fend for herself, picking up jobs to support her mother while excelling in school. She was determined to become a lawyer, so she could fight for the underprivileged and protect those who couldn't protect themselves.

Then there was **_Nisha, the quiet one of the group_**, but her silence spoke volumes. Nisha was the type of girl who could get lost in a book for hours, her dark brown hair always tucked behind her ear as she scribbled down notes in the margins of her notebooks. Her large brown eyes carried a sense of wonder and curiosity that no one could ignore. Nisha's love for reading had led her to study literature and journalism. She dreamed of becoming a writer, telling the stories of the unheard, the unnoticed, and the overlooked.

Her journey was one of self-discovery, finding her voice in a world that often wanted her to remain silent.

Meera, the artist of the group, had the kind of beauty that radiated from within. With long, curly auburn hair and deep hazel eyes, Meera was known for her creativity and unique vision of the world. She was the one who could take a simple idea and turn it into a masterpiece. Growing up in an affluent family, she never had to worry about money, but she struggled with the pressure of being perfect. Meera's parents expected her to follow a traditional path in life, but she longed to break free and pursue art. Over the years, her love for painting had grown, and she knew that she wanted to use her art to bring about social change, to challenge the norms that society had imposed upon her.

Then there was ***Tara, the sportswoman***. With her short, platinum blonde hair and bright blue eyes, Tara had always been the one who never gave up, no matter the odds. She had a natural gift for athletics and had been the star player of her school's basketball team. But Tara had a deeper story than her athletic achievements. She had grown up with a disability her left leg had been amputated when she was younger due to a medical condition. Tara had never let that stop her; in fact, it fueled her determination to prove that no obstacle was too great. She wanted to become a motivational speaker, inspiring others who faced similar challenges to pursue their dreams and believe in themselves.

The last member of the group was ***Ayesha, the tech prodigy***. With short, pixie-cut hair and a constant glimmer of curiosity in her eyes, Ayesha was the tech genius. She had been fascinated by computers since she was a child, and by the time she was sixteen, she had already developed her first app. Growing up in a conservative family, Ayesha's passion for technology had not always been understood or supported. But she didn't let that deter her; instead, she worked tirelessly on her coding skills, determined to make a name for herself in a world that didn't always welcome young women in tech. Ayesha dreamed of one day building her own tech startup, creating innovations that would improve lives and bridge gaps in society.

These five girls were inseparable. They had met in high school, and their friendship had flourished through shared experiences of struggle, triumph, heartbreak, and growth. Together, they created a sisterhood that no one could break. They pushed each other to be their best selves, held each other up during their darkest times, and celebrated each other's victories, no matter how small.

One day, Zara came up with an idea that would change everything. *"We need to do something,"* she said, gathering the girls at their usual spot, a small café near the town square. *"We all have our dreams, but why not combine them? We can build something together. Something that empowers not just us, but every woman out there."*

The girls listened, intrigued, as Zara shared her vision. *"What if we create a platform, a community where girls can learn from each other, support each other, and build the courage to follow their dreams? We could provide scholarships, offer mentorship, and create a network that connects girls from all walks of life. We could be the change we want to see."*

The idea hit them all like a lightning bolt. They knew it wouldn't be easy, but they also knew they were capable of it. Each of them had a unique strength, and together they had the power to make something incredible happen.

Nisha, with her love for writing, would be in charge of content creation. She would share powerful stories of women who had broken barriers and followed their dreams, inspiring others to do the same. Meera would use her art to create the visual identity of their platform, creating designs and illustrations that captured the essence of empowerment. Tara, with her athletic background, would bring in fitness programs and motivational talks, showing girls how they could push through obstacles, both physical and mental. Ayesha would be the tech genius behind the platform, building a website and app that would allow girls to connect, share resources, and access mentorship from women in various fields. Zara would be the leader, the one who would take charge of the organization and ensure that everything ran smoothly.

The group worked tirelessly over the next few months, putting their all into this project. They faced numerous challenges along the way, from lack of funding to technical issues to societal pushback. But each time they stumbled, they picked each other up and kept moving forward. They applied for grants, reached out to mentors, and used their own savings to get the project off the ground.

Finally, after months of hard work and dedication, ***their platform, EmpowerHer,*** was launched. It started as a small online community, but soon it gained traction. Girls from all over the world joined, drawn by the stories, the resources, and the promise of a space where they could be themselves and chase their dreams without fear of judgment.

EmpowerHer wasn't just about career advice or academic success it was about holistic empowerment. It was a place where girls could learn to love themselves, embrace their flaws, and support each other. It was a place where girls could be encouraged to step into their power, to be bold, to speak up, and to go after what they wanted.

As the platform grew, so did the girls. They faced challenges that tested their resolve, but they always stuck together. They had created something that was bigger than themselves, a legacy that would last long after they were gone. They had proved that when women supported each other, there was no limit to what they could achieve.

Years later, the five girls stood together, now successful in their respective careers, but forever tied by the sisterhood they had built. They had empowered thousands of young women to follow their dreams, break barriers, and embrace their inner strength. And they knew that this was just the beginning.

Because when women rise together, there's nothing they can't do.

15
Shadows of Revenge

In a bustling city filled with towering buildings, neon lights, and endless streets, two men once inseparable Adrian Stark and Damien Holt had become bitter rivals. Their friendship, forged in childhood, had slowly transformed into something much darker over the years. They had once shared dreams, ambitions, and an unspoken bond. But now, the very bond that held them together had shattered into pieces, leaving a trail of anger, betrayal, and a hunger for vengeance.

Adrian Stark: The Charismatic Entrepreneur

Adrian Stark was the type of man who could walk into a room and command attention. With his sharp blue eyes, perfectly tailored suits, and quick mind, he was the epitome of success. He had built a multi-billion-dollar tech empire focused on artificial intelligence, a company that dominated the market. Everyone knew him as the golden boy the one who had it all: wealth, fame, and influence. But Adrian's desire to be the best had come at a high cost, one that would soon haunt him.

Damien Holt: The Brooding Genius

Damien Holt was Adrian's former friend, now his greatest enemy. Where Adrian thrived in the spotlight, Damien had always preferred the shadows. A genius in technology and hacking, Damien used his mind to control the digital world. His dark, brooding appearance and quiet demeanor only added to his mystique. He had spent years honing his skills, waiting for the right moment to strike back at the man who had betrayed him. That moment was coming.

Their rivalry began years ago, when Adrian, in a moment of weakness, made a decision that would tear their friendship apart. The two had been working on an innovative technology that could revolutionize the tech world. But when a lucrative deal came up, Adrian chose to accept an offer from a powerful corporation, leaving Damien out of the equation entirely.

Damien, who had trusted Adrian like a brother, was devastated. The betrayal was more than just business it was personal. And for years, Damien worked in the shadows, plotting his revenge.

One evening, Adrian sat in his high-rise office overlooking the city. His empire was thriving, but something felt off. His phone rang. The number was unfamiliar. He answered it.

"Stark," he said, his voice cool.

A deep, calm voice responded. *"We need to talk."*

Adrian froze. He recognized the voice immediately. It was Damien.

"Damien," Adrian said, his voice tensing. *"What do you want?"*

"I want to bring you down," Damien said, the coldness in his voice sending a chill down Adrian's spine. *"And I will. It's only a matter of time."*

Adrian stood up from his desk, his mind racing. *"You're still bitter about that deal, aren't you? Get over it. It was just business."*

"Business?" Damien scoffed. *"You left me behind. You betrayed me. And now, I'm going to make you regret it."*

Adrian's hands clenched into fists. *"You can't take me down. I built this empire. I've worked harder than anyone to get here."*

"You're wrong," Damien replied. *"I've been planning this for years. Everyone has a weakness, Adrian. And I've found yours."*

Adrian's heart raced. *"What do you mean?"*

"You'll see soon enough," Damien said cryptically before hanging up.

The call ended, leaving Adrian in stunned silence. The fear that he had never experienced before began to set in. Damien wasn't just seeking revenge he was coming for everything Adrian had built.

In the following weeks, Adrian's life spiraled into chaos. His company was hit with cyberattacks small at first, but they quickly escalated. Systems crashed, sensitive data was stolen, and private information leaked. Adrian's team worked tirelessly to patch things up, but every time they thought they had solved the problem, another breach occurred.

And then, one night, Adrian received an encrypted message.

Meet me at the old warehouse by the docks. Midnight.

Adrian knew it was a trap. But he also knew it was the only way to confront Damien. He had to face him head-on.

At midnight, Adrian arrived at the warehouse. The lights were dim, and the air was thick with tension. He heard the distant echo of footsteps and stepped further into the cavernous space, heart pounding.

And then, from the shadows, Damien appeared. He was dressed in all black, his eyes gleaming with an eerie calm.

"You're late," Damien said, his voice low.

Adrian didn't respond right away. His eyes scanned the space, taking in the dark corners and empty shelves. *"What do you want, Damien?"*

"I want to watch you lose everything," Damien said with a twisted smile. *"I want to see you fall from your pedestal, just like you made me fall."*

Adrian clenched his fists. *"You think this is going to make you feel better? Destroying my company? You think that'll fix anything?"*

Damien's expression hardened. *"It's not about feeling better. It's about justice."*

Adrian took a step forward, his voice filled with quiet anger. *"You've spent years hiding in the shadows, plotting your revenge. But I'm done with this. I'm going to stop you. I don't care what it takes."*

Damien's smile faltered. *"You're too late."*

With a swift motion, Damien pressed a button on his phone. Suddenly, the warehouse lit up with screens showing live footage of Adrian's company in crisis. The damage was already done. Adrian's empire was in ruins.

"You've lost, Adrian," Damien said coldly.

Adrian stood there, seething. *"You've been planning this all along, haven't you? All these years, just waiting for the right moment."*

Damien nodded, his face twisted in satisfaction. *"You never saw me coming."*

Just when Damien thought he had won, Adrian's phone buzzed. It was a notification from his system.

A backup plan that he had secretly prepared years ago kicked in. Adrian had anticipated that someone, one day, might try to destroy everything he had worked for. So he had built an AI-driven fail-safe system into his company, something that no one, not even his closest team members, had known about.

The screens in front of them flickered and went black. Damien's face twisted in confusion. *"What... how?"*

"You thought you could beat me by destroying my systems," Adrian said, his voice steady. *"But you didn't consider the backup plan. You never thought I'd be prepared for you."*

The warehouse fell into silence. Damien's victory was slipping away, and he didn't know how to stop it. Adrian had outsmarted him.

For a long moment, neither man spoke. Damien stared at Adrian, his face filled with disbelief. He had thought he could win, thought that his years of planning would finally take Adrian down. But Adrian had anticipated everything.

"You're right," Adrian said softly. *"We were once friends. But I don't want to fight anymore. I've lost too much. Let's end this."*

Damien's expression softened just a little. The tension in the room dissipated, and for the first time in years, he felt something other than anger. It wasn't forgiveness, not yet. But maybe, just maybe, they could start over.

Adrian turned to leave, knowing that this wasn't the end of their story it was just the beginning of a new chapter.

As the warehouse doors creaked open, Adrian stepped into the night, feeling lighter than he had in years. The battle wasn't over, but for the first time, he felt like it might finally be possible to end the war.

16
The House on Hollow Hill

The wind howled through the narrow alleyways as the **old town of Ashford lay** shrouded in an eerie mist. Towering trees bent with age lined the roads, their skeletal branches reaching out like twisted fingers. On the outskirts of town, there was a house that locals spoke of in hushed tones a house that had stood empty for decades but had never truly been forgotten.

It was a **mansion perched on Hollow Hill**, hidden behind overgrown vines and a forest of thick, dark trees. The house was once grand, its tall windows now boarded up, and its crumbling façade whispered secrets of a bygone era. Most people avoided it, and those who didn't would often regret it.

Eliza and her younger brother, Jacob, had just moved into Ashford, searching for a fresh start after their parents' tragic death in a car accident. They weren't prepared for the unsettling atmosphere of this small town, nor for the legend that followed the house on Hollow Hill.

One night, unable to sleep, Eliza stood by her bedroom window, staring out into the darkness. The house was just visible in the distance, its silhouette casting an imposing shadow against the moonlight. Jacob had heard rumors from the local children about the house being haunted. They claimed that at night, strange noises echoed from inside creaking floorboards, faint whispers, and even ghostly figures could sometimes be seen through the windows.

Her curiosity got the better of her.

"Jacob," she called softly, waking him from his sleep, *"I need to see that house. It's all anyone talks about around here."*

Jacob groaned but agreed reluctantly, his fear evident on his face. *"It's not a good idea, Eliza. We don't know anything about it. The people here, they're... different. And weird things happen around that place."*

But Eliza had already made up her mind. She was tired of the mystery haunting her thoughts.

They bundled up, and with a flashlight in hand, they set off toward Hollow Hill under the cover of darkness. The closer they got, the colder it seemed to grow. The wind picked up, and the hairs on Eliza's neck stood on end.

When they reached the foot of the hill, Eliza noticed something strange there were no animal sounds, no chirping crickets, not even the rustle of leaves. Just silence. It felt unnatural. A sense of dread washed over her, but her curiosity pushed her forward. They reached the wrought iron gates that surrounded the property, their once gleaming black paint chipped and flaking away.

The gate creaked open with a disturbing groan as they pushed it forward.

The mansion loomed ahead, its dark windows like dead eyes watching them. The front door, barely hanging on its hinges, was open, as if inviting them inside. The smell of mildew and rot wafted through the air, mixing with the thick, heavy atmosphere. Eliza hesitated for a moment before stepping across the threshold, and Jacob, though terrified, followed.

"Eliza... this isn't right," Jacob whispered, his voice shaking. *"We should leave."*

But Eliza, determined to uncover the truth, pressed on. The house seemed to respond to their presence. The old wooden floorboards groaned under their weight as they moved deeper into the darkness. Every shadow seemed to stretch unnaturally, every creak too loud, too deliberate. The air was thick with a dampness that made it hard to breathe.

As they ventured further inside, they found themselves standing in what appeared to be the main hall, its large staircase leading up to the second floor. But the real horror lay in the walls themselves. There were strange markings, symbols carved into the wood and stone, fading but still visible. Eliza reached out to touch one, and her fingers tingled with an electric shock, as though the very house itself was alive and watching her.

"I don't think we should be here," Jacob insisted again, his voice now louder, filled with fear.

But Eliza ignored him, her mind fixated on the eerie house. The floor below them shifted, and a sudden loud bang echoed through the house. They froze, their hearts racing.

A voice faint but unmistakable whispered through the darkness. *"Leave... now... while you still can..."*

The voice was cold, hollow, like a long-forgotten memory. It sent a wave of terror through Eliza, but she couldn't bring herself to leave. Instead, she stepped forward, her heart pounding in her chest.

"Who's there?" she called, her voice trembling.

For a long moment, there was nothing. Silence, thick and suffocating.

Then, from the darkness above them, a figure appeared at the top of the stairs. A woman, her pale face framed by long, disheveled hair. Her eyes were wide, unblinking, and her lips stretched into a twisted smile.

"Leave... now..." the woman whispered, her voice like the scratching of nails on a chalkboard.

Jacob grabbed Eliza's arm. *"We need to go, NOW!"* His fear was palpable, his grip tight as he tried to pull her away.

But Eliza, in a trance, didn't move. Her eyes were locked on the woman. She felt something in her that she couldn't explain some connection, some strange pull.

The woman's smile widened. *"You've come for me... finally,"* she said, her voice growing louder, filled with malicious joy.

Suddenly, the house seemed to come alive. The walls groaned, the floor trembled beneath their feet, and the temperature dropped drastically. Eliza felt an icy hand brush against her cheek. The woman's figure began to fade, but not before her words echoed through the house, chilling them to the bone.

"Your blood will be mine."

In an instant, the lights flickered and the doors slammed shut. The entire house seemed to shake with an overwhelming force. Eliza turned to run, but her legs wouldn't move. Jacob was crying out, pulling her with all his might, but it felt as though they were trapped in a nightmare, unable to escape.

The figure of the woman reappeared in front of them, her eyes glowing with an otherworldly light. *"You are not leaving. You will never leave. The curse is upon you."*

The air grew colder, and Eliza's breath became visible in front of her. Then, she saw it her reflection in a cracked mirror on the wall. But it wasn't just her. There was something else... a shadow, standing beside her.

She gasped, realizing too late that the woman wasn't just a ghost. She was a presence, a force that had been bound to this house, this cursed place. And now, it had chosen Eliza to take its place.

The last thing Eliza heard before everything went black was Jacob's scream, and the echo of the woman's voice as it faded into the darkness:

"Welcome home, my dear."

17

From Dark Shadows to Bright Light

In a small, forgotten village nestled between mountains, lived a boy named **Ravi**. His life began in a house built of tin and cardboard, surrounded by dirt roads that wound their way through the barren landscape. His family was one of many struggling in the village, where hope was scarce and survival was a daily struggle.

Ravi had no illusions about his future. He knew that at best, he would end up working the fields like his father, a man whose hands were worn and cracked from years of hard labor. His mother, ever kind-hearted, dreamed of a better life for him, but even her dreams were weighed down by the burdens of poverty.

When Ravi was just seven years old, his mother died, and his father became a shell of the man he once was. Grief consumed him, and Ravi was left to care for him as best as he could, despite his young age. But as time passed, the village began to change. A construction company set up shop in the area, and workers flooded in from across the region, bringing new opportunities and ways of life that Ravi had never seen before.

One day, Ravi overheard a conversation between the workers. They were discussing a scholarship program for children of poor families, a way to help them escape the cycle of poverty. The details were vague, but something in Ravi's heart clicked. This was his chance.

However, he didn't know how to apply. He couldn't even read or write. He barely even knew how to use a computer. But the dream of getting out, of building a life for himself outside the confines of his village, fueled him. He knew what he had to do.

For the next few months, Ravi borrowed books from the workers when they were done with their shifts. He spent his nights learning to read, learning to write, teaching himself the skills he'd need to even begin to dream of a future outside the village. He sat under the dim light of his father's old lamp, pouring over books about the world he'd only heard of in stories: faraway cities, bustling markets, schools filled with students like him, all free to dream.

Ravi's determination caught the attention of a **teacher named Aisha**, who had recently been hired by the construction company to help the village children learn. She noticed his growing passion for education and offered to help him with his application for the scholarship. But there was one obstacle: the deadline was fast approaching, and Ravi still wasn't ready. He didn't know enough, and he feared it was too late for him.

But Aisha believed in him, and together, they worked day and night. Slowly, Ravi's writing skills improved. His handwriting, once messy and disjointed, grew neat and precise. His understanding of the world expanded as Aisha introduced him to new subjects, ones he had never heard of before.

The day of the application arrived, and Ravi was ready. He submitted his form, along with an essay he had written about his dreams. But Ravi couldn't escape his fears. What if he wasn't good enough? What if he failed like so many others before him? The self-doubt crept in, but he pushed it aside, choosing instead to focus on what he had accomplished, rather than what he hadn't.

Weeks passed, and the waiting began to take a toll on him. Ravi worked harder than ever in the fields to take his mind off the anxiety. He cared for his father, still lost in his grief, and never once complained. It was all he knew work, survival, perseverance.

Then, one fateful day, Ravi received a letter. It was from the scholarship committee. His heart raced as he tore it open. The letter was short, but it held the weight of his entire future:

"We are pleased to inform you that you have been selected for the scholarship. Your hard work and determination have earned you the chance to attend school in the city. Congratulations, Ravi."

Ravi couldn't believe it. He had won. A wave of emotions crashed over him. He had done it. He had broken free.

But with the joy came the weight of a decision. Ravi knew that in order to pursue his dreams, he would have to leave his father behind, a man who had once been his world, but now could barely function without him. His father, once so full of life and hope, had become a shadow of his former self, too immersed in his own sorrow to see the possibilities before him.

For weeks, Ravi struggled with the decision. He wanted to go, to take the opportunity that had been given to him, but his father needed him. But life had a cruel way of forcing decisions, and one day, Ravi realized that his father wouldn't survive without him. And the only way to help him was by showing him that there was more to life than the pain of the past.

On the day Ravi left for the city, he found his father sitting by the window, staring into the distance, lost in his grief. Ravi knelt before him, holding his father's hand, and said, *"I have to go, Papa. But I'll never forget you. I'll always come back. You taught me to fight, to never give up. And now, it's my turn to fight for us, for you. I'll make you proud."*

His father's eyes flickered with something hope, maybe. It was the first time in years that Ravi saw his father's eyes soften, and for a moment, it felt as if everything would be okay.

Years passed.

Ravi moved to the city, where he studied tirelessly, earning a degree in technology. He started working with a startup company, applying all the knowledge he had learned from his time at the shelter and in the fields. Ravi's ambition and hard work began to pay off, and within a few years, he was not only a successful entrepreneur but a philanthropist as well. He founded his own non-profit organization aimed at helping children in rural areas receive an education.

But despite his success, Ravi never forgot his roots. He continued to support his father from afar, sending money and occasionally returning to the village to visit. His father, though still grieving the past, had slowly found his own sense of purpose he began working at a local school, mentoring children and helping them realize their potential.

Ravi's story became one of inspiration, a reminder that success wasn't defined by wealth or status but by the ability to overcome obstacles and give back. As his company flourished, Ravi made it his mission to help others rise from the ashes of their circumstances, just as he had.

In the end, Ravi Matthews didn't just escape the poverty that had defined his youth he created a legacy of hope, a beacon for others to follow. From the dusty streets of his village to the heights of success, Ravi showed the world that even the smallest spark of hope could light up the darkest corners of the world.

18
Tunnels of Valor

Captain Arjun Rathore had always known that the path of a soldier was fraught with danger, sacrifice, and emotional strain. But he had never anticipated the gravity of the situation that now lay before him. A sudden and deadly attack had struck deep within Indian territory, and his battalion was among the first to respond. Yet, the danger wasn't just the enemy forces they were facing an entirely different kind of battle, a struggle against treacherous terrain, unpredictable elements, and an intelligence network so deeply embedded, it would take more than brute force to overcome it.

The first obstacle they encountered was the terrain craggy mountains, dense forests, and unpredictable weather. It was a region that had always been difficult to navigate, and now, in the dead of night, the Indian forces were going in blind. The air was thin at high altitudes, making it hard to breathe, the snowstorms so fierce that visibility was reduced to just a few feet.

Arjun, however, knew better than to let his men feel fear. His experience had taught him that in the face of nature's wrath, only one thing would keep them moving forward: resilience. He moved forward, leading his men through the storm, ensuring that each footstep was taken carefully, calculated, and deliberate.

"Follow my lead," Arjun called over the roar of the wind, his voice steady. *"Step where I step. Keep your heads low, and don't lose sight of the goal."*

Lieutenant Neha Kapoor, a sharp and trusted officer who had served under Arjun for years, kept close by. Despite the storm, she never faltered. But even she could feel the weight of the situation. They weren't just fighting for survival now. They were fighting for the safety of their families, their country, and the future of those who couldn't fight for themselves.

After hours of trudging through the snow, they finally reached the edge of the forest where the enemy's base had been reported. It was deep within enemy territory, a place that was carefully guarded and hidden by rugged terrain and a series of secret tunnels. What Arjun hadn't expected was the enemy's heavy reliance on these underground passages hidden routes, almost forgotten by most, that allowed the enemy to move troops and supplies without being detected.

These tunnels had long been abandoned by their own side due to the difficult nature of navigating them, but the enemy had found a way to use them against the Indian forces. It was a piece of intelligence that had been left unchecked, and now it was too late.

"We've got to move quietly. There's a network of tunnels beneath this area," Arjun warned his team. *"The enemy's using them for supply routes, but we can't risk them escaping underground."*

The group began to search for the entrances to the tunnels, moving slowly through the dense forest. The risk of alerting the enemy was high, and Arjun was keenly aware of how dangerous it could be. The last thing they wanted was a shootout in the heart of the enemy's domain far from reinforcement and with no way of communicating to base.

Finally, Neha spotted an entrance hidden beneath a canopy of tangled roots, concealed by a sheer drop at the edge of a cliff. The entrance was so well camouflaged that it almost seemed like an illusion. It was a perfect hiding spot, and they had nearly walked past it. Arjun signaled for the team to halt. His heart raced. They had found their way in.

The tunnels were dark and narrow, but they were also a lifeline. Arjun's men moved carefully, crawling through the low-ceilinged corridors, as the sounds of the forest faded behind them. It was eerily silent, the only noise coming from the echo of their boots on the stone floors. It was in these tunnels that the real battle would begin. The enemy had secured a large cache of weapons hidden beneath the ground, and Arjun's mission was simple: disrupt their plans, prevent further attacks, and gain intelligence that could help their forces strike back decisively.

However, there was one more thing Arjun hadn't anticipated: the place was rigged with explosives booby traps that would kill anyone who triggered them. He realized that the enemy had anticipated any breach into their base and had created a maze of death to protect it. They would have to maneuver through a series of puzzles and traps to reach the enemy's stronghold.

"Be careful," Arjun whispered to his team. *"These tunnels are booby-trapped. Keep your eyes open for anything suspicious."*

Neha crouched low, studying the stone walls, her sharp eyes scanning for any unusual markings or objects. The team moved cautiously, with every step calculated. There was no room for error.

As they delved deeper into the tunnels, the heat became oppressive, the air thin, making every breath feel like a battle. The darkness closed in around them, but Arjun's sense of determination kept them moving. He couldn't afford to let his men feel the weight of the situation. They had to remain focused on their mission.

Suddenly, there was a loud click. The unmistakable sound of a trap being activated.

"Down!" Arjun shouted, throwing himself to the ground, signaling for his team to do the same. A split second later, a barrage of sharp metal rods shot from the walls, narrowly missing them. Arjun's heart pounded in his chest. They had just dodged a lethal trap.

"That was too close," Neha muttered, her breath shaky.

"Keep moving," Arjun ordered. *"We're almost there."*

With his eyes never leaving the path ahead, Arjun led the team through the winding tunnels, using his knowledge of military strategies to predict what might lie ahead. Finally, they reached the core of the enemy's supply base. The men and equipment were less than thirty feet away. There was no time to waste.

When they reached the heart of the base, the enemy soldiers were caught off guard. Arjun's platoon struck with the force of a storm fighting their way through armed guards, disabling the weapons caches, and sending a clear message to the enemy. It was a fight not just for survival but for honor, for justice.

As Arjun faced off with the leader of the enemy unit a man who had orchestrated these attacks he felt his heart burning with anger. It wasn't just about victory anymore. It was about stopping an enemy that had crossed too many lines.

In a fierce exchange of gunfire and hand-to-hand combat, Arjun finally disarmed the enemy leader. Holding the man at gunpoint, he spoke the words that had been burning in his chest since the mission began.

"This is for my men. For Vikram, for all of us who've sacrificed everything to protect what we hold dear."

The mission was a success, but at a cost. Many lives had been lost, and the physical toll on Arjun's body was immense. Yet, in that moment, he knew they had achieved something far greater than just defeating the enemy. They had safeguarded their people, their country, and their legacy.

As Arjun stood in the aftermath of the battle, he looked up at the sky clear, calm, and vast. The storm had passed, the enemy had been defeated, but the real victory lay in the strength of his team, their courage, and the promise that they would always fight, no matter what the odds. And as they returned to base, walking through the same snow-covered terrain they had fought so hard to conquer, Arjun knew that the true test of their courage was not just in the fight, but in carrying the spirit of honor and sacrifice forward for future generations.

This was not just a victory on the battlefield. It was a victory for the soul of the nation, a testament to the unbreakable bond of duty, and the unwavering courage of the men and women who had fought for it.

19
The Silent Witness

Detective Ayaan Malik was called to a crime scene on a rainy night in Mumbai. The body of a famous blind pianist, **Meera Sood,** was found lying on the floor of her upscale apartment. She was still sitting in front of her grand piano, her fingers frozen on the keys. There were no signs of struggle, no forced entry. It looked like an accident, a tragic slip while she was playing her final piece. But Ayaan wasn't buying it. His instincts told him something didn't add up.

Meera Sood was known for her hauntingly beautiful performances, and the city's elite adored her, even though she was blind. Her ability to *"see"* the emotions of the music made her performances unique, and it drew people in. But now, in her final moments, Ayaan was convinced there was more to her death than meets the eye.

Ayaan stood over her lifeless body, his eyes scanning the scene. Meera's apartment was luxurious, with expensive furniture and ornate paintings hanging on the walls. But one thing caught his attention a video recorder on the piano. It was still running. Ayaan played the tape.

Meera was visible in the recording, sitting before the piano, playing a beautiful, melancholic tune. But just as she finished the piece, a figure appeared in the doorway. The door opened quietly, and Ayaan watched as a man walked toward her. His face wasn't clear, but the sound of his footsteps was distinct.

"Who's there?" Meera asked, her head turning in the direction of the footsteps.

The man didn't speak. He took a step closer to her.

The last thing the camera recorded was the faint sound of a struggle, a muffled gasp, and then silence.

The Investigation Begins......

Ayaan set to work, starting with the basics. He learned that Meera had been involved with a rich businessman, Sameer Verma. Sameer had been a regular at her performances, often sitting in the front row. Ayaan's first instinct was to speak to him, but the man was out of town for a business meeting. His alibi checked out, but Ayaan couldn't ignore the connection. Was Sameer in town the night of the murder? Was he involved?

But things weren't as clear-cut as they seemed.

Ayaan's next lead took him to **Rhea, Meera's close friend and personal assistant**. Rhea seemed devastated by Meera's death, offering no resistance as Ayaan questioned her. But there was something off. Rhea seemed to know a little too much about Meera's life, her relationships, and even the details of the murder that weren't public yet.

"I don't understand," Rhea said, her voice wavering, *"How could she be gone like this? She was always so careful. She told me she feared someone might hurt her..."*

"What do you mean? Who would want to hurt her?" Ayaan pressed.

Rhea hesitated for a moment, then spoke slowly. *"Meera had been receiving strange letters. Anonymous ones, warning her. She didn't say much, but... I think she knew someone was watching her. That someone might harm her."*

This sent Ayaan's mind racing. Meera had been receiving threats. Had it been Sameer, or someone else?

As Ayaan dug deeper, he discovered something unsettling. Meera had been recording a secret series of performances, different from her usual concerts. These were personal, private recordings where she played pieces that seemed to convey a hidden message. It was as if she were trying to tell a story through her music. One of the recordings was labeled *"The Final Piece."*

Ayaan listened to it. The melody was tense, almost frantic, like Meera was trying to warn someone. Then, suddenly, he heard a strange noise in the background, a voice whispering softly, but unmistakably clear: *"Don't play it, Meera. You're being watched."*

It wasn't Meera's voice. Ayaan rewound the recording, his heart pounding. The whisper was faint but there. Ayaan traced the source of the recording to a hidden compartment in the piano. There, he found a small, hidden microphone. Someone had been spying on her.

Ayaan's investigation led him to a shocking conclusion. The figure in the video wasn't just any man. It was Rhea, Meera's close friend and assistant. The twist: Rhea had orchestrated the entire thing. She had been feeding Meera false information, manipulating her into thinking she was being watched, all while carefully orchestrating her death.

But why? Why kill Meera?

It turned out that Rhea had been having an affair with Sameer Verma. Meera, unknowingly, had become a threat when she discovered their secret. She had planned to expose their relationship and had even started to play a new song that hinted at their affair. Rhea couldn't risk it. She couldn't let Meera ruin everything. So, she staged the entire scene, pretending to be a concerned friend while secretly plotting her death.

And the biggest shock came when Ayaan discovered that Meera's blindness was not entirely natural. She had feigned it. Meera had perfect vision until a few years ago, when she decided to blind herself in a symbolic act to *"see the world differently"* a deliberate choice to detach herself from reality. But the real reason? To gain sympathy and attention, all while continuing to manipulate the people around her, including Sameer and Rhea.

Rhea, realizing she had been caught, tried to flee, but Ayaan was one step ahead. He had already notified the authorities, and she was arrested. Before she was taken away, Rhea looked at Ayaan with a calm, almost amused expression.

"You think you understand everything, Ayaan?" she said, her voice laced with bitterness. *"You're just like Meera. Always playing your little game, thinking you're in control. But none of us are in control."*

Ayaan stood still, staring at her as she was led away. The final note in Meera's life, the one that had seemed so symbolic, now felt hollow. The truth was far more complicated than anyone could have imagined.

As he walked away from the crime scene, Ayaan couldn't shake the feeling that he had just uncovered the tip of the iceberg. There were always more layers to peel away, more games to be played. And this case, much like life, was far from over.

20
Breaking the Chains

Aarohi had known nothing but the sting of anger and the weight of harsh words from a very young age. Her childhood was defined by the constant sounds of shouting and the violence that followed. Her father, a man consumed by frustration and his own failures, found a target in his daughter. For the smallest things, from a missed pencil to a spilled glass of water, he would raise his hand to punish her. The love that should have surrounded her was replaced by fear and silence.

Aarohi's mother, Meera, loved her deeply, but she, too, was a victim of the same abusive cycle. She couldn't protect her daughter from her husband's wrath, as she, too, was often the subject of his violence. But despite all the suffering, there was something in Aarohi that never broke her will to rise above the darkness of her environment. As she grew older, she became quiet, observant, and resilient, learning to endure and navigate the turbulence of her home life.

When Aarohi entered high school, the weight of societal expectations started to suffocate her. Her teachers, friends, and relatives all insisted that she pursue arts, telling her that it was the best fit for her, simply because she was a girl. They said that science and medical studies were not meant for people like her. It was the way things were supposed to be. She was expected to quietly follow a path of lesser dreams, one where girls didn't need ambition, and their dreams were limited.

But Aarohi wasn't the kind to follow anyone's rules, least of all the ones dictated by outdated traditions. While others tried to convince her that she should accept the role of a quiet, docile girl, Aarohi was already dreaming of bigger things. Despite the pressure, despite the constant emotional and physical toll from her home, she found herself making a decision that no one saw coming.

She chose medicine.

Her mother, who had always stood by her through thick and thin, supported her decision. *"You can do anything, Aarohi,"* Meera said, wiping the tears from her eyes. *"Don't let anyone tell you what you're capable of."*

With the emotional support of her mother, Aarohi began her journey in the medical field. She worked tirelessly, studying late into the night, often using her passion for music as a way to unwind. She would sing softly to herself when the weight of the world felt too heavy. Her voice, her only escape from the harshness of her life, gave her comfort. She began singing at local events and clubs, her voice reaching more people than she could ever imagine.

In the face of adversity, Aarohi not only excelled in her studies but also became one of the top students in her medical degree program. She achieved first place in her class, a testament to her resilience and the strength of her spirit. But her success came at a cost. Even though her father's cruelty had always been a part of her life, it didn't stop the undercurrent of negativity from others, too. Her success wasn't celebrated, but instead, it was met with jealousy, resentment, and constant criticism. She was too **"ambitious"** for a girl, they said. They said she was getting ahead of herself, living a life that girls weren't supposed to dream of.

But Aarohi kept going. She didn't stop for anyone. She completed her post-graduate studies in medicine, becoming a doctor a young woman with a dream far too big for anyone to contain. At the same time, her passion for singing continued to grow. She performed on stages across the country, her soulful voice touching hearts everywhere she went.

But despite her success, the environment at home never changed. Her father's anger only grew, and his bitterness toward her accomplishments and dreams deepened. Her relatives looked at her with disapproval, as though she had betrayed her place in the world. They never saw her as a success they only saw a girl who was out of line, a girl who had refused to be **"tamed."**

However, none of their words could stop her from becoming who she was destined to be.

Years passed, and with her growing medical career, Aarohi slowly built a life for herself, one that was free from the chains of her past. She bought her mother a beautiful house, far away from the suffocating atmosphere of their old home. Meera finally got the peace she deserved. Aarohi made sure to surround her mother with everything she needed, from doctors to a comfortable life where she could finally rest after all the years of suffering.

Aarohi's success became the ultimate answer to the criticism she had faced. With each new milestone, she silenced the voices that had told her she couldn't do it. With each stage she performed on, her confidence and power grew. No longer was she the timid, beaten-down girl from a broken home she was a symbol of defiance, strength, and hope.

Her father, the man who had once beaten her for every little mistake, now stood in the shadows of her life, nothing more than a fading memory. Her relatives, the ones who once scoffed at her ambitions, now had no choice but to acknowledge her success. Aarohi had become a woman who not only broke free of the chains that had bound her but also gave her mother a life of dignity and love.

One evening, as Aarohi stood on stage, singing her heart out to a sea of adoring fans, she thought about how far she had come. She thought of the little girl who had cried herself to sleep, hoping for a way out of the pain. She thought of her mother, who had given everything to support her, even when no one else did. Aarohi smiled to herself, knowing that this moment was more than just a performance. It was her victory, not only over the world that had tried to put her down but over the parts of herself that had once been broken.

"This," she thought as she sang the final note, *"is for us."*

Aarohi had proven that no matter where you come from, no matter the odds stacked against you, you could rise. And for her, that was the sweetest melody of all.

21

Rise, Unbroken

From shadows cast, where silence lay,
A girl once lost, now finds her way.
Through storms of rage, through tears of night,
She learned to stand, to find her light.
The chains that bound, the words that hurt,
She wore them all, but didn't shirk.
For deep inside, she knew her worth,
A fire burning bright from birth.
Her voice was soft, but fierce in song,
A melody that made her strong.
No dream too wild, no path too steep,
She climbed the heights, though others weep.
They said, "You can't, you're just a girl,"
But she stood firm, and let them swirl
In their own doubts, in their own hate,
While she wrote her own, unspoken fate.
From broken home, to stage she rose,
A tale of strength the world now knows.
With every note, with every stride,
She fought, she soared, she turned the tide.
Her journey long, her road so tough,
But she was more than enough.
The scars of pain, the weight of blame,

She wore them like an honored name.
For in her heart, no fear could stay,
She'd turn the night into the day.
Empowered now, she owns her soul,
No longer bound by others' toll.
Rise, unbroken, stand your ground,
In every silence, hear your sound.
The world may try to tear you down,
But you're the queen who wears the crown.
In your heart, there's no retreat,
You are the storm, you are the beat.
Empowered, fierce, and set alight,
You are the dawn, you are the fight.

22

NOTE

I hope you enjoyed the stories across different genres, each crafted with originality and a unique twist. I aimed to reconnect with diverse emotions, experiences, and dreams through these narratives. From overcoming adversity to unraveling mysteries, every tale was meant to spark thought and reflection. Thank you for reading, and may these stories ignite your imaginative interest in their own special way.

Whispers Of Wisdom: Quotes To Inspire And Reflect

A collection of thoughtful reflections that speak to the heart, encouraging growth, kindness, and the pursuit of authenticity.

"In the tapestry of life, every thread of challenge weaves a pattern of strength."
Life's challenges may seem like knots or tangles in the grand design, but over time, they contribute to the creation of something beautiful. Each struggle, big or small, adds resilience, and through them, we become more whole.

"True wisdom lies not in knowing all the answers, but in embracing the beauty of the questions."
Wisdom isn't about having every answer at your fingertips it's about having the courage to ask the right questions and the patience to understand that some answers come with time. The pursuit of understanding is often more valuable than certainty.

"Hope is the gentle breeze that keeps our dreams afloat amidst life's storms."
Even when the world feels heavy and the winds of adversity blow hard against us, hope is that quiet force that lifts us up. It gives our dreams the resilience to survive through the darkest of times, reminding us that the storm will eventually pass.

"Kindness is the universal language that transcends all barriers and unites humanity."
No matter where we come from or what language we speak, kindness is the thread that binds us all together. It doesn't need translation—its message is always understood, and its impact always felt. In a world full of differences, kindness is the common ground we all share.

"Growth begins at the edge of comfort, where courage meets the unknown."
True personal growth happens when we step outside our familiar surroundings and face what we fear. It's in these moments of discomfort and uncertainty that we discover new strengths and unlock potential we never knew existed.

"The heart's compass always points toward authenticity; follow it to find your true north."

When you listen closely, your heart always knows the way. In a world that often pushes conformity, following your true self is the most powerful journey you can take. Authenticity is your inner guide, leading you toward fulfillment and peace.